Thespian Playworks 2011

The Goatman Cometh
by I.B. Hopkins

Eisegesis
by Nick Mecikalski

See You Soon
by Morgan Richardson

Clipped
by Sam Van Wetter

A SAMUEL FRENCH ACTING EDITION

FOUNDED 1830

SAMUELFRENCH.COM

MUSIC USE NOTE

Licensees are solely responsible for obtaining formal written permission from copyright owners to use copyrighted music in the performance of this play and are strongly cautioned to do so. If no such permission is obtained by the licensee, then the licensee must use only original music that the licensee owns and controls. Licensees are solely responsible and liable for all music clearances and shall indemnify the copyright owners of the play and their licensing agent, Samuel French, Inc., against any costs, expenses, losses and liabilities arising from the use of music by licensees.

IMPORTANT BILLING AND CREDIT
REQUIREMENTS

All producers of *THE GOATMAN COMETH, EISEGESIS, SEE YOU SOON,* and *CLIPPED must* give credit to the Authors of the Plays in all programs distributed in connection with performances of the Plays, and in all instances in which the titles of the Plays appear for the purposes of advertising, publicizing or otherwise exploiting the Plays and/or productions. The names of the Authors *must* appear on a separate line on which no other name appears, immediately following the title and *must* appear in size of type not less than fifty percent of the size of the title type.

ABOUT THE COVER

Photographs on the cover of this publication were taken at the Thespian Playworks staged readings in June, 2011. Actors pictured are:

The Goatman Cometh: Griffin Sutherland as Dr. Eliot and Celi Oliveto as Glorianne.
Eisegesis: Jesse Beam as Man 1.
See You Soon: Rachel Shippee as Girl and Adam Novas as Boy.
Clipped: Mark Devine as Petey and Kirstin Lynch-Walsh as Elise.

FOREWORD

Pain.

That's one thing these four very different plays have in common—and it isn't just the characters who suffer, in their diverse quests for love, knowledge, and reconciliation. Each of the student writers behind these award-winning scripts has known the agony, the "wincing struggle," as Isaac Hopkins expressed it to me in a recent e-mail, "of tearing open the carcass of a draft for the purpose of rearranging its organs."

I think we have a new Thespian Playworks mission statement!

Kidding aside, these four teenaged authors have learned, in an environment we try to make welcoming and safe, what most playwrights discover in the much harsher world of the profession: bringing a new script to life *hurts*.

"For me the hardest thing was coming to grips with the fact that it could be improved," confessed Nick Mecikalski, whose *Eisegesis* had already won another contest before being named a Playworks finalist, earning Nick a ticket to the 2011 Thespian Festival for a week of workshop rehearsals and staged readings. "I'd gotten into the mindset that I was done with it." And then he found himself in a University of Nebraska classroom with director Mark D. Kaufmann, dramaturg Max Posner (a two-time Playworks alumnus, now a working playwright), and a company of student actors, who all had their own ideas about Nick's harrowing interrogation drama centered on a bright young physicist.

"They really dissected my play," said Nick, now a senior at Bob Jones High School in Madison, Alabama. "I learned so much."

The same proved true for I.B. Hopkins (*The Goatman Cometh*), from Gainesville High School in Georgia; Sam Van Wetter (*Clipped*), of Denver School of the Arts; and Morgan Richardson (*see you soon*), a graduate of Enloe High School in Raleigh, North Carolina, now at Fordham University.

"It was really great to collaborate with professionals who could open my eyes to things I maybe wasn't seeing," Morgan reflected. "Once you realize that it's all geared toward making (your play) the best it can be—from that perspective, it's not as painful."

Sponsored annually by the Educational Theatre Association and run by the staff of *Dramatics* magazine, Playworks was launched in 1994 as a tribute to longtime International Thespian Society executive Doug Finney. Samuel French, Inc. has been a major supporter of the program since

2009, and this anthology, the second of its kind, should relieve any lingering anguish among Nick and his fellow Playworks finalists. For us at *Dramatics*, knowing these talented young people as we do and hoping to see their work on many more stages in the future, it's a great source of joy, excitement, and pride.

 "There's pleasure and hope in writing something that you know is just you," Sam Van Wetter said. "Playworks showed me that this 'me' is doable. It's feasible and it's stageable and it gets people going. I can't tell you how valuable that is."

Yeah: feels good.

—Julie York Coppens
Associate Editor, Educational Theatre Association
February 19, 2012

CONTENTS

THE GOATMAN COMETH

by I.B. Hopkins

THE GOATMAN COMETH was originally produced on November 16th, 2010 at Gainesville High School's "Warehouse" in Gainesville, Georgia as the final phase of *The Escape Triad*. It was directed by Isaac Hopkins. The Artistic Direction was Pam Ware. The cast was as follows.

LEILIA ELIOT.. Madeline Harr
DOCTOR ELIOT..Isaac Hopkins
PATRICK..Chris Hallows
MRS. GLORIANNE HARRIS... LaKeisha Ligon
THE GOATMAN.. Greg Bryant

THE GOATMAN COMETH was produced at a part of Thespian Playworks at the University of Nebraska, Lincoln on June 26, 2011. The play was written by I.B. Hopkins of Gainesville High School in Gainesville, Georgia and was presented by the Education Theatre Association and *Dramatics Magazine*. It was directed by Phillip W. Moss, with dramaturgy by Erica Saleh. The cast was as follows:

LEILIA ELIOT .... Genna Guidry
DOCTOR ELIOT .... Griffin Sutherland
PATRICK..Ryan Maltz
MRS. GLORIANNE HARRIS .... Celi Oliveto
THE GOATMAN..Avery DiUbaldo

ABOUT THE PLAYWRIGHT

Isaac "I.B." Hopkins is a native of Gainesville, Georgia. He is the youngest son of Marsha and Benjie Hopkins and is sibling to Boone, Mayes, and Ethan Hopkins. Isaac graduates from Gainesville High School in the spring of 2012, and he plans to pursue the arts of writing and of theatre in college and beyond. In addition to *The Goatman Cometh*, he has authored eight other one-act plays.

CHARACTERS

LEILIA ELIOT - Teenaged and trapped.

DOCTOR ELIOT - Mysterious man who keeps to himself.

PATRICK - Teenaged and love-struck as though by a two-by-four.

MRS. GLORIANNE HARRIS - A lady about the town and the wife of a butcher.

THE GOATMAN (Ches McCartney) - A marauding mystic who appears to have been birthed by the very mountains.

SETTING

Stairs up to a porch at right. Furnished living room/parlor set at right with sofa, chairs, side tables, and all other playthings needed to keep a home are set at left. The space has very much a sense uncertainty with little sense of depth.

The color is green. Jade. Beryl. Willow. Forest. Grass. Sea. Kelly. Lime. Olive. Sage. Pea. Spinach. Chartreuse. Malachite. Verdigris. Moss. Pine. Sap. Fir.

Appalachia swirls about the scene as a tilt-a-whirl.

A NOTE ABOUT THE PLAY

The character Ches McCartney is roughly based off of an actual person who traveled with a herd of goats throughout the United States, mostly in the rural South. He sold junk items, preached, and marauded for more than 50 years but was forced to retire after a brutal mugging in Los Angeles in 1987. Known as the "Goatman," he found his way into the hearts and legends of generations of Southerners. He was rumored to have been as old as 120 years when he died in a nursing home in Macon, Georgia, in 1998.

Scene 1

(**LEILIA** and **PATRICK** *sit on the porch at right. An awkward adolescent love is clearly blossoming between them in spite of the painful barrier of their contretempts.* **PATRICK** *is frustrated with his own lack of assertiveness; maturity betrays* **LEILIA**'s *youth. They lounge comfortably together.*)

LEILIA. *(unconvincingly)* No.

PATRICK. Aw, c'mon. Just tell me.

LEILIA. I'm not going to tell so I don't know why you keep on asking.

PATRICK. I promise I won't tell a soul.

LEILIA. It's not even interestin'. It's not even really worth telling, and just as soon as I do tell you, you're going to say the same thing—it wasn't worth the labor of getting it out of me.

PATRICK. Now, Leilia. We, both of us, know that you're gonna tell me eventually. It's all a matter of how long we're gonna keep talkin'.

LEILIA. We can keep on straight through the night, and I'm still not.

PATRICK. You won't let anybody close enough to think that you might be just a little vulnerable, will you?

LEILIA. Really, it doesn't matter…

PATRICK. I told you. I don't care. I want to know.

(*After a moment,* **PATRICK** *pushes* **LEILIA** *off the cliff.*)

LEILIA. All right. Fine. So it started out with just me walking down through the woods to the branch out behind the house. Everything looked normal to me until I got down to the water. It looked like somebody had thrown up some kind of platform real hastily. Like a little stand for looking at the creek. And right in the middle of it was a... *(pause)* bathtub. Just out in the middle of Creation. And there was a girl about our age sitting in it looking just as pleasant as she could.

PATRICK. In a bathtub? Was she naked?

LEILIA. Well, yeah. Far as I could tell. But it's not like there was any water in the bathtub; it was just filled up with all kind of little colorful candies. She just kept on sitting there and grinning.

PATRICK. That all?

LEILIA. No. Then I went on walking down to the stand, you know, to go and ask her what she was doing down there, but when I started to climbing up, it started a-creaking and shaking real hard. And finally it just broke apart and got picked up by the river. So there I was just staring as it all floated on down river. The stand, the bathtub, the girl, and all the little colored candies...floating away downstream.

PATRICK. Then what?

LEILIA. What do you mean "then what"? I woke up after that.

PATRICK. *(teasing)* That was it? Shoot! That wasn't even worth the labor of getting out of you.

LEILIA. Patrick, you go home. You go home right this instant. I won't have you making fun of me like that.

PATRICK. Aw, you know I'm only just kidding. That was... *interesting.*

LEILIA. Well?

PATRICK. Well?

LEILIA. Well.

PATRICK. Weeeeeellll.

LEILIA. Tell me what it means. You said you could tell me what my dream meant; now tell me.

PATRICK. Now I told you I *might* be able to tell you what it meant. I don't really know. I have a few ideas but nothing that makes a whole lot of sense.

LEILIA. What's the matter? Is Mr. Fortune Teller afraid to show any real feelings of his own?

PATRICK. I never said—

LEILIA. Scared you might look vulnerable?

PATRICK. That's not it.

LEILIA. Then just say it!

PATRICK. *(after a moment)* Your eyes look different today. Not bad. Just different. Pretty.

LEILIA. Patrick, look at me. Quit changing the subject and tell me what you think.

PATRICK. Fine. I think… I think you might have some *feelings* you're not talking about.

LEILIA. *(drawing up from her reclining position)* What is that supposed to mean?

PATRICK. Nothing. It didn't mean a thing.

LEILIA. What kinds of feelings am I supposed to not be talking about?

PATRICK. I don't know. Can't we just drop it?

LEILIA. No. I know what you're doing. You think you know something about me that I don't know. And…well…I want to know.

PATRICK. Well…it's just…do you remember last week when I shared my M&M's with you?

LEILIA. Yeah.

PATRICK. I told you I'm probably wrong, but I think you see yourself as the girl in the bathtub and me as the M&M's.

LEILIA. You didn't tell me anything except you won't melt in my hand. What does it mean?

PATRICK. Well, Leilia. You know we've known each other for a while now, and I just think that you might… might…

LEILIA. Might what?

PATRICK. That you might have started to have some—

(Brassily, **MRS. GLORIANNE HARRIS** *enters from right. She appears a little shaken even through her iron-pursed lips. Never has* **PATRICK** *been gladder to see this woman's starkly floral-print dress appear to relieve his guard duty.)*

GLORIANNE. My stars! My stars! *(a bit out of breath)* Leilia? Leilia, run fetch the Doctor for me. *(not giving her time even to stand)* Well, go on, child. Get!

LEILIA. Mrs. Harris, I thought you knew. The Doct—

GLORIANNE. Patrick? Patrick boy, what are you doing hanging around here? You're supposed to be in town at the store, I'm sure of it.

PATRICK. I just figured, seeing how Wednesday is always our slow day and how Mr. Harris was still there, I might be able to take off a little early. So I come to see Miss Leilia.

GLORIANNE. Oh, I see. You figured you could leave early so you did.

PATRICK. Well, yes, ma'am.

GLORIANNE. Boy, I've tried to give you a chance in the world, and you go and spit in my face. No, I don't want to hear it. You go on and get your sorry back-end back to the shop, and if you can't find nothing else to do, organize the deep freeze.

PATRICK. But, Mrs. Harris, he's surely closed up by now anyway.

GLORIANNE. You don't want to argue with me right now. You don't.

PATRICK. But couldn't I just—

GLORIANNE. *(pointedly)* What did I just say?

PATRICK. Yes, ma'am.

(He gets up to leave but lingers for but a moment looking at **LEILIA.** *)*

Bye, Leilia. We'll talk later.

GLORIANNE. Now!

(He leaves, sapling that he is.)

LEILIA. Bye, Pat. *(a beat)* Good ev'ning, Mrs. Harris. How's business?

GLORIANNE. Are you deaf, child? Didn't I tell you to fetch the Doctor?

LEILIA. Oh, Mrs. Harris, I thought you knew. The Doctor isn't seeing anybody for a few weeks. He calls this his hibernation.

GLORIANNE. I don't care. I don't care. Tell him it's Glorianne and it's an emergency.

LEILIA. I really don't think I can do that, ma'am. He told me right out that I shouldn't let anybody in.

GLORIANNE. Am I not making myself clear?

LEILIA. He said not to come after him…even if it's Glorianne and an emergency.

(GLORIANNE makes a sudden movement of her arm. LEILIA cringes, expecting to be struck. It turns out to just be a foreboding little frayed oriental fan.)

GLORIANNE. I'm not going to say it again, child.

LEILIA. *(relenting)* Yes, ma'am.

(LEILIA crosses left to within.)

(GLORIANNE falters. Her pimento is without an olive. She paces, sitting occasionally only to stand a half-second later.)

GLORIANNE. *(Now alone, she fans herself to excess.)* Oh God! Oh. Oh God. Harold what have you done? *(having had a moment to inspect her surroundings)* Uggh! I swear they keep this place a pigsty. I doesn't matter what time of year I climb my bones up onto this porch; it's always filthy with dry leaves. It doesn't kill a soul to pick up a broom now and again. *(She grabs one from up and begins to sweep with unwarranted fury.)* A little freshness always does some good. No matter how grubby things get, there's all the time some clearing out that helps. It doesn't do anything to just let bad things alone—they fester.

(The **DOCTOR** *comes out from left. He carries a hand-kerchief lightly, making no pretence about his perceived importance. His speech is languid, confident— as are his eyebrows.)*

DOCTOR. Was your emergency hygiene-related, Glorianne?

GLORIANNE. No, and don't you go patronizing me. I'm here on quite a serious call.

DOCTOR. *(chuckling to himself)* I'm sure.

GLORIANNE. Oh, you're gonna repent your words when you hear.

DOCTOR. What can be so plaguing you, Glorianne?

GLORIANNE. What? Out here? Where the wide world can hear? Are we heathens?

DOCTOR. Would you care to come inside?

GLORIANNE. I'd be obliged.

(He gestures for them to cross into the parlor. The furniture here is almost notably erratic but not quite. **GLORIANNE** *sits, posing dramatically, on a divan or the like at left.)*

DOCTOR. Well...?

GLORIANNE. Oh! Oh, it's worse than I've ever let myself think it could be.

DOCTOR. *(hollowly)* I can't bear the suspense.

GLORIANNE. Doctor, you are going to rue your words. Ooh, how you'll rue 'em. I just can't wait to see your face!

DOCTOR. I was napping, Glorianne...

GLORIANNE. Well, I'm not entirely certain how to say this... It's not like me to nose around, but... *(screwing up her nerve)* Harold is having an affair.

DOCTOR. Harold? Your Harold?

GLORIANNE. *(overwhelmed)* It's true. It's true. I never though this sort of thing would happen, but here it is before me...

DOCTOR. Now, Glori. Are you sure you're not just jumping to conclusions? Sometimes no matter how we try to put a thought away, we see it everywhere.

GLORIANNE. No, no. I'm certain of it. Whenever he thinks I'm out for awhile he'll wash 'til he raws up his skin and soak his collar with that godawful cologne. Then he shows up in the next morning and won't look me in the eye. He just goes on and mutters something about playing cards in the back at Stipe's.

DOCTOR. I don't know what I can tell you. I suppose you've come to me for some comfort, a portion of solace, but I don't know what good—

GLORIANNE. Oh, I don't want you to tell me it's going to be all right. That's not why I came here.

DOCTOR. Isn't it?

GLORIANNE. I want some help getting even.

DOCTOR. I really can't help you do that in good conscience.

GLORIANNE. Of course, you can. He's wrong, ain't he?

DOCTOR. Yes, but—

GLORIANNE. *(standing as a raptor)* Well then, he ought to be punished. I don't mean just shouting and crying and sleeping on the couch and divorce. I mean I want him to *sweat* it out.

DOCTOR. Is that really rational?

GLORIANNE. Yes, it most certainly is. Now help me think— what could I do to get him back for his faults?

DOCTOR. I'm not going to take part in this mischief.

GLORIANNE. Personally, I think the punishment should fit the crime…

DOCTOR. Glori, think about what you're saying!

GLORIANNE. I did hear that the Goatman was coming to town. He should be here in just a couple days…

DOCTOR. Is he? I wonder where he'll set up camp.

GLORIANNE. *(scheming)* Well, Harold will be leaving tomorrow for another one of his "fishing trips." Maybe I ought to invite him to pass the night at our house. We don't have an extra bedroom, but I'm sure I could find something to do with him…

DOCTOR. Don't even start down that road, Glorianne. That man is decent and would never stoop so low. He is a preacher— I hope you realize.

GLORIANNE. I'm sure he is. That's why I'm sure he'd be all too glad to oblige me.

DOCTOR. *(rationally)* I can't believe *you'd* even consider such a thing. You still don't even have any real proof that Harold has been a...that he's been unfaithful.

GLORIANNE. You know I'd hoped a man in your position might be a little wiser.

DOCTOR. And in what position exactly is it that I am?

GLORIANNE. You are supposed to be shrewd. *(renewing her soap opera-learned dramatic air)* But I can see that if you were, you would not be trying to upset me while I am in this fragile state!

DOCTOR. *(calm as Edvard Grieg)* Glorianne.

GLORIANNE. I know. I know the way out.

*(The **DOCTOR** escorts **GLORIANNE** back out of the parlor and onto the grimy porch.)*

DOCTOR. *(sighing)* You just care too much. Harold really is a lucky man, you know. He'll realize it; don't worry.

GLORIANNE. Lucky doesn't even begin to describe what he is...

*(He has guided **GLORIANNE** in finding her way contemptibly back onto the porch only to notice **PATRICK** sketchily sounding out the Eliot home.)*

GLORIANNE. Boy, I swear. I am not gonna be able handle your not minding to me.

PATRICK. I haven't done a thing wrong.

GLORIANNE. What's the matter with you? You're not even making good sense.

DOCTOR. Glori, why don't you go on home, and I'll send the boy along shortly.

GLORIANNE. *(taking her leave)* All right, fine. But I swear on all that's good and holy if that deep freeze isn't spotless by the time we open shop in the morning, I'll send you in to clean it and won't let you back out again.

PATRICK. I'm sorry, Doctor, but I just have to see Leilia again before I go on back.

DOCTOR. I'm sure you do.

PATRICK. So...can I go up and see her?

DOCTOR. No, no. I don't believe so.

PATRICK. *(taken aback)* What? Why?

(The **DOCTOR** *entirely disregards his questions. After a heavy beat, he inhales deeply.)*

DOCTOR. There's not a thing we can do to slow spring from coming or to speed it up. It's always the same, but I'm still never ready for it.

PATRICK. I don't understand why I can't just run see her for just a minute.

DOCTOR. *(sizing the boy)* Has the spring come already? Can't the young keep their hearts a little longer?

PATRICK. Sir, please just talk to me. *(a beat)* At least tell me why I can't see her.

DOCTOR. She wants a lot. Ensure that you won't disappoint.

PATRICK. *(stammering through his discomfiture)* I...we're not even...it's not like that.

DOCTOR. But you wish it were?

PATRICK. Well, yeah. But, see, I have no idea if she...she might...I think she might...but I don't really know... And I don't really feel comfortable talking with you about this sort of thing...

DOCTOR. You're not going to see her tonight, and I would suggest that you return only when you have a more substantial hold on the situation.

PATRICK. That's not really—

DOCTOR. Now I believe you need to run on home, Patrick. After all, you have an early morning at the butcher shop ahead of you.

(**PATRICK** *begins to protest before reluctantly turning to leave.*)

PATRICK. Goodbye, Doctor. And tell Leilia goodnight for me, too.

DOCTOR. No.

(**DOCTOR** *re-enters his home.*)

Interlogue 1

(The most silent of hour of the night. The parlor at left is dimly lit to chiefly show silhouettes. A noiseless figure, the **DOCTOR***, enters and goes about methodically rearranging the room's furnishings. When he has completed his somber task, he leaves just as deafly as before.)*

Scene 2

(Lights come up on the successive morning to find **LEILIA** *alone. She reads some worn book with pointed interest, her legs crossed under her. A single finger rests gently on her temple.)*

(She looks up suddenly startled as though having heard a disturbance. Turning back to her novel, she disregards whatever it was. After a moment **DOCTOR** *enters from his study; the even atmosphere freezes.)*

LEILIA. Oh. I'll go.

(She makes to do so in dejection but just before she reaches the door is caught by the **DOCTOR**'s *interjection.)*

DOCTOR. I'd rather you didn't.

LEILIA. Is there something you need?

DOCTOR. No, nothing in particular.

LEILIA. Then why did you come out?

DOCTOR. I just thought maybe we ought to talk. I believe it'll do you some good. It may even do me some good.

LEILIA. So you think you can just come out here and suddenly we can talk like everything is normal.

DOCTOR. I had hoped so, yes.

LEILIA. *(sitting again, now annoyed)* Fine. What are we talking about?

DOCTOR. *(wispily)* Oh, I don't think that matters very much at all. Something tells me we can be talking about anything at all in the world and still be talking about the same thing—specifically. What are you reading?

LEILIA. What do you care?

DOCTOR. Just answer me…please.

LEILIA. Fine. It's *1984.*

DOCTOR. Ah. *(quoting)* "War is Peace. Freedom is Slavery. Ignorance is Strength." I always liked that book. It makes you think. What is truth? And is it worth risking the perils of questioning authority…

LEILIA. Yeah, and it only ever makes people question more.

DOCTOR. So it does.

LEILIA. Nobody knows what's really *real.* They want truth.

DOCTOR. Truth is relative. Read Einstein.

LEILIA. They're always going to want to know more; they deserve to understand.

DOCTOR. Do they?

LEILIA. *(standing)* Yes! Even when people are in the dark they always keep feeling around for the light switch.

DOCTOR. Even if they harm themselves in searching. Falling over unseen obstacles.

LEILIA. *(indicating the novel)* Apparently.

DOCTOR. So then what? What happens in the novel? What becomes of our plighted hero Winston Smith?

LEILIA. I…I don't know. I haven't finished the book yet.

DOCTOR. Well, I'm afraid I'll be ruining it for you. In the end Winston Smith is happy. He's happy—not because he knows anymore than he did before but because he doesn't, and he doesn't want to anymore. *"Ignorance is Strength."*

LEILIA. *(a rigid beat)* I'm sick of your metaphors. Why can't we just talk…really talk? I never honestly talk with anybody. It's always these elusive "theys" in symbolically darkened rooms!

DOCTOR. *(His ostrich head still in the sand.)* What shall we talk about?

LEILIA. Are you serious? Tell me the things you know I want to know! Who am I? I *don't understand.* Why am I living here? Are you my father, my grandfather? Are you just some man? My whole life I can only ever remember living here with you and not knowing why. You can't just not tell someone where they came from—

DOCTOR. *(correcting her)* From where they came.

LEILIA. Where they came from and expect them to be okay with that. Nobody will tell me anything, and I don't even know what to say when people ask simple questions about me. It's like I can't even really exist until I know certain things—certain things that only you can tell me. But you won't. You're a monster, and you won't.

(The **DOCTOR** *looks ready to relent for a moment before hiding again.)*

DOCTOR. I'm sorry, but you have to trust that I know what I'm doing. You must think I'm an awful person.

LEILIA. Yeah. I do.

DOCTOR. I intend to tell you when you're grown, you should know.

LEILIA. Well, then it's a good thing you can keep me an ignorant child as long as you don't tell me then.

DOCTOR. The child is clever.

LEILIA. I hate you.

DOCTOR. You do now.

(From off right we hear a scuffle. A grappling struggle appears to be going on and fast approaches the porch. It is **PATRICK** *and a hairy, rather uncombed man who could pass for any age. They are engaged in a mobile sort of tug-of-war over what appears to be the* **GOATMAN** *'s staff of a walking stick.)*

GOATMAN. Get ya off of me, boy!

PATRICK. Don't you take another step, old man.

GOATMAN. I said you need to get on out of my way!

PATRICK. You stay away from Miss Leilia. Now git on!

GOATMAN. I'll get on my way when I please. Now if you don't unhand me and let me by, I swear to the good Lord Jesus—

PATRICK. You'll what?

GOATMAN. I'll teach you to mind!

(The **GOATMAN,** *making good, proceeds to wriggle the staff from* **PATRICK** *and use it to pelt the boy. He recoils as* **LEILIA** *and the* **DOCTOR** *work their way hurriedly out on to the porch.* **LEILIA** *makes a point to linger at the door in the presence of this stranger.)*

PATRICK. *(nursing his abrasion)* Ah! You're crazy, old man! You're just what they say you are.

GOATMAN. And what's that they say?

PATRICK. That you're crazy! No people can stand to be around you so you keep the company of goats.

GOATMAN. I have no pity for a sinner as you.

DOCTOR. Ches! It's so good to see you again.

GOATMAN. Doctor, Doctor. I hardly recognized you.

DOCTOR. Surely I've not changed too much.

GOATMAN. Only your nature.

DOCTOR. *(slightly blighted)* And you have not. Where are your things?

GOATMAN. I'm parked in the pasture 'round back. I do appreciate you letting me stay there. I'll only be here shortly.

DOCTOR. You're welcome to stay as long as you please.

GOATMAN. Much obliged.

DOCTOR. Ches, there's no need to be too rough with Patrick. He's harmless really.

GOATMAN. *(to* **PATRICK***)* I hope I didn't hurt you, son.

PATRICK. *(defensively)* I'm fine.

GOATMAN. C'mon, let me take a look at you.

PATRICK. I said I'm fine!

DOCTOR. *(reprimanding subtly)* Why don't you come with me, Patrick, and we'll have a look at you? *(gesturing the* **GOATMAN** *inside)* Ches, please make yourself at home.

(As the **GOATMAN** *is led to cross left inside, the* **DOCTOR** *takes* **PATRICK** *by the elbow to sit him down on the porch steps.* **CHES** *and* **LEILIA** *are left alone. The following should be played as independent scenes that happen to coincide, moving back and forth, a pendulum.)*

GOATMAN. I don't believe we've been introduced. M' name is Ches McCartney.

LEILIA. *(still tentative)* I'm Leilia Eliot. It's nice to meet you, Mr. McCartney.

GOATMAN. Oh, everybody just calls me Goatman—well, everybody except the Doctor, of course.

LEILIA. And why is that?

DOCTOR. Where do you get off harassing strangers like that? Huh? Answer me.

PATRICK. If you'd heard what I heard about him you'd of—

DOCTOR. I've heard plenty. More than you, I'm sure. Haven't you ever heard of not believing everything you hear?

PATRICK. *(resolutely)* I thought he might be after Miss Leilia.

GOATMAN. Oh, I'd say it's because I've been travelin' around with a herd of goats past 40 years.

LEILIA. Just you and the goats?

GOATMAN. Just me and the goats. We keep each other company. We even keep each other warm.

LEILIA. Excuse me?

GOATMAN. Yupp. Come winter there's not a thing to keep the chill away like sleepin' in a pile of goats.

PATRICK. I heard 'em talking in town about him. They said he rolls into town and makes friendly for a few days then he makes off with the prettiest girl he can find.

DOCTOR. *(all eyebrows)* Is Miss Leilia the prettiest girl he could find, Patrick?

PATRICK. Well, I think so.

DOCTOR. The people from whom you heard those awful lies—and yes, they are lies—are simply afraid of someone being a little different than they are. They're scared of not knowing something.

PATRICK. How can you be sure?

LEILIA. Well, that's *interesting*.

GOATMAN. You know— you remind me of myself.

LEILIA. Do I?

GOATMAN. *(searching for his collar somewhere in the grime)* Yup. When I was a young man, I was a mighty dapper fellow, hard as that may be to believe. I was always willing to work, of course; I just didn't like the getting all dirtied up 's'all. I kept my clothes and face clean as best I could ever since I was just a little fellow. But one day when I'd took up work for the WPA all that sorta foolishness stopped mattering. We'd been working long hours at all the rough work of clearing roads. A buddy of mine was assigned to chopping trees with me. Neither of us had looked where we were standing or where the tree would fall. Long and short, the last thing I saw was a 50 foot sequoia land straight on me—full on.

DOCTOR. Glorianne was right; you do have a little smart *mouth*. I can be sure because I know the man. I trust him. I invited him to stay with me at my home, didn't I? Are you questioning my judgment, Patrick?

PATRICK. I just…I don't understand.

DOCTOR. That's the difference. I don't see that as a problem. You need to learn the virtue of trust.

PATRICK. *(begrudging)* Yes, sir.

DOCTOR. Good. *(a pause)* I can see that you are still quite fond of Miss Leilia.

PATRICK. *(grinning now)* Yes, sir.

LEILIA. So what happened?

GOATMAN. *(simply)* Well…I died.

LEILIA. Ohh?

GOATMAN. I suppose I should say I like to have died. I was knocked out so cold they brung down a mortician from Canada. They went all about getting ready to bury me as one of the casualties of the New Deal. If I hadn't of woke up 3 days later in the morgue, I'd've actually needed to be there.

LEILIA. They were fixin' to bury you?

GOATMAN. All but. Anyhow, from that experience of coming so close to Jesus afore my time, I, everyday since then, have not given a worry to providin' for my appearance. I know I'll be provided for just as the lilies of the field.

LEILIA. That's mighty noble of you. But I still believe a good bath never offended any good Christian. Especially Jesus.

PATRICK. Doctor Eliot?

DOCTOR. Hmm?

PATRICK. How long is this goatman gonna be staying around here?

DOCTOR. Oh, I'd guess for as long as he feels welcome.

PATRICK. Then shouldn't he have already left?

(GLORIANNE storms furiously on to the porch. She clearly has been bawling, but she would rather appear bundled up in her coarse rage-rug to mask her blunder of character.)

GLORIANNE. Boy, I know I do not see you at this house again. I'm sure I do not see you doing just what I told you not to do.

DOCTOR. I'll be with you in a moment, Mrs. Harris.

GLORIANNE. *(snapping at him)* I'm not talking with you this time.

DOCTOR. I see. Patrick, you had better go.

PATRICK. Can I say goodbye to Miss Leilia?

DOCTOR. I don't think that's a very good idea.

PATRICK. *(as he runs in to the parlor against the Doctor's orders)* Leilia? Leilia? Leilia, I have to go.

LEILIA. Okay.

PATRICK. Bye.

LEILIA. Bye.

GLORIANNE. *(ushering him off abrasively to the right)* Boy, get on back. Straight back. No stopping on the way. And you're not coming back here, you hear me?

DOCTOR. I take it you confronted Harold.

GLORIANNE. I'm tired of you ripping my life up to pieces. I'm leaving.

DOCTOR. I'd rather you didn't. Mr. McCartney is here, you know.

GLORIANNE. The Goatman? Here? *(Not waiting for an invitation, she crosses into the parlor.)* Mr. Goatman? Mr. Goatman, please keep your seat. It is so lovely to make acquaintance with you. I have heard so many lovely things.

GOATMAN. I'm flattered, ma'am.

DOCTOR. Ches, this is Mrs. Glorianne Harris. She and her husband have a butcher shop in town. Finest one in the county.

GOATMAN. It's a pleasure to meat you, Mrs. Harris.

GLORIANNE. Oh, please. Just call me Glori.

(Her smile gleams sharply as lights fall.)

GOATMAN. Well alrighty then, Glori.

GLORIANNE. You know, Mr. Goatman, every time you come to town, I think myself. I think, "Self, you need to get down and go see that lovely Goatman they're always talkin' about."

DOCTOR. *(savoring)* Aren't you glad, then, that you've had the chance now. I guess you were leaving though. Shame that. I wish you could sit a spell with us, but we understand and will be sure to have you over again soon.

GLORIANNE. Now hold on a minute. I'm not going anyplace. How often is it that a simple countrywoman gets to make acquaintance with a celebrity?

GOATMAN. Oh, I'm just like the next fella, after all.

GLORIANNE. *(parrying)* Don't you go and sell yourself short now! I'm mighty in'rested though, how is it that you met the Doctor here? I knew that you were a friend, but I was never real clear on just *how* you two know each other...

DOCTOR. We simply made acquaintance. Glori, it's what people do. Kind of like how you two just met. Imagine that.

GLORIANNE. Why don't you just tell the story anyway?

GOATMAN. I hardly remember, truth be told.

LEILIA. (*becoming aware of herself, her physical mass*) Just tell the story.

DOCTOR. There's no need for all that, Leilia.

LEILIA. I'd just like to know.

GLORIANNE. No reason not to.

GOATMAN. Righty-o. There's no harm in that. The goats and me and…we was passing through these parts one afternoon quite a number of years ago now. I was just a wandering along when an old woman…what was her name?

DOCTOR. I believe it was Mrs. Dot Small.

GOATMAN. That's it. Anyhow, she called me over to where she was settin' on her porch. She took pity on us. She told me I should go see the Doctor, that I needed a bath and a sturdy meal before I got back on the road again. Long and short, I did.

DOCTOR. I invited Ches to stay with me, and he did.

GOATMAN. And rarely have I known such hospitality or friendship. He opened up his home to me at a time when I needed it most.

LEILIA. So…was I even born yet when you were staying here?

GOATMAN. I can't quite recall…

DOCTOR. You were very small, an infant. You wouldn't remember.

LEILIA. I wouldn't know.

GOATMAN. I do seem to recall a child. A baby. Ah, yes. I remember. You…you were a lovely child.

DOCTOR. Ches, you have quite a memory about you suddenly.

GOATMAN. It photographic. It just never got developed.

GLORIANNE. She must have been quite a special child for you to remember that, then Mr. Goatman.

GOATMAN. She was. I guess she is now, too.

DOCTOR. You'll make the child blush, Ches.

LEILIA. Thank you.

Interlogue 2

(same as Interlogue 1)

Scene 3

(The parlor, now rearranged once more, is shown as lights come up. Several days have passed, little having changed. **LEILA** *sits again in her chair with her legs crossed under her and her finger resting lightly on her temple. This time, however, she reads no book but is engrossed in a conversation with the* **GOATMAN** *who sits a short distance away. Captured.)*

GOATMAN. …and, well, somebody had to keep that grizzly from gettin' to town. It fell to me, I suppose. It didn't take real long to track it, but when I did, I didn't have no gun on me.

LEILA. What did you do!?

GOATMAN. I just had to scrap with him. I knew he could've tore me to shreds at any moment but had to keep on. I just knew I couldn't let him go and get after any more folks so I kept on. I finally was able to get a hold of a big stone and crack him over the skull. I came back to tell the man at the circus that his bear was dead, but he didn't seem to care too much. He just grinned real big and offered me a job as a sideshow bear wrestler.

LEILA. Did you take it?

GOATMAN. I sure did. Anybody'd take any job back then. But I didn't wrestle bears for too long. What I ended up as was the assistant in a knife show. Had a dozen knives thrown at me 5 times a day by a Spanish maiden.

LEILA. Well, why would you do that?

GOATMAN. *(a pause, then as if it should have been obvious)* Because I loved her. It took quite a while, mind you, before I could round up enough courage to even talk to her. Everybody knew the world's strongest man was sweet on her. I was scared.

LEILA. Did you ever tell her you loved her?

GOATMAN. I sure did. Eventually. And one night we just eloped off together. Had to.

LEILA. Didn't you miss everybody, all the people you knew?

GOATMAN. Sometimes I did. Sometimes I still do, but I don't guess I could ever get past needing to be out on the road.

LEILIA. You've had so many adventures.

GOATMAN. You call 'em adventures. I call 'em gettin' by.

LEILIA. But it's better than this.

GOATMAN. Than what?

LEILIA. Than all this. Than my whole life. I'm all blindfolded because no one wants to tell me anything. I've got nothing for me here.

GOATMAN. You have the Doctor.

LEILIA. He's the main problem.

GOATMAN. You have that Patrick boy. He loves you.

LEILIA. He doesn't love me like that. He's just a good friend, and he's a little bit annoying sometimes anyway. I just want to be free and on the open road. There I can see and understand and know what things are about.

GOATMAN. Now you're dreaming. You have a beautiful life here.

LEILIA. No, I don't. *(a moment to think)* You should let me go out on the road with you. We could travel all over together. We could have adventures.

GOATMAN. *(laughing off the absurdity)* Do you want to smell like a goat for the rest of your life? You don't want to come on the road with me.

LEILIA. I can't stay here.

(Clearly having to swallow his nerves every few seconds, **PATRICK** *enters on to the porch from right. He is wrought with anxiety in his ill-fitting, sickly patterned suit. He is quite simply a teenage boy "ready" for a date. He knocks on the door.)*

LEILIA. Oh, no! I forgot!

GOATMAN. What?

LEILIA. *(frantically standing)* It's Patrick. I forgot I told him I would go to the dance with him.

(He knocks again.)

LEILIA. Oh, I hate this. I didn't even get a dress.

GOATMAN. You'd better go find something to put on.

(another knock)

DOCTOR. *(from off)* Will someone please answer the door!

LEILIA. I got it.

*(She goes and answers the door. Seeing that she is not dressed, **PATRICK** enters the parlor. His crest falls instantly.)*

LEILIA. *(a pause)* Hey.

PATRICK. What are you doing? You said we would go to the Spring Fling together. Why aren't you dressed yet? Am I early? I must just be a little early because I know you wouldn't just stand me up like this. I know you wouldn't, Leilia. You're not like that. You're not like other people.

LEILIA. Listen, Patrick. I just sort of got caught up here and forgot all about the dance. I'm really sorry. If you want, I can go find something to wear.

PATRICK. No. That's not what I wanted anyways. Forget about the dance. Well, I guess you already did.

LEILIA. Pat, I am so sorry. I don't know how I can make it up to you.

GOATMAN. I can think of a way.

PATRICK. No. I said it's fine.

LEILIA. I really don't know why you wanted to go to that dance anyway.

PATRICK. Why wouldn't I?

LEILIA. Well, the people who go to those dances aren't exactly yours or my kind of people. It's not worth going to see them.

PATRICK. *(a beat)* It's not about those people.

LEILIA. Then what's it about? You needing to go to a dance?

PATRICK. No! It's about you. It's about getting to go to the Spring Fling with *you*, or it was.

(**LEILIA** *is silent for longer than would be comfortable or expected. Weary of the icy quiet,* **PATRICK** *simply leaves.*)

GOATMAN. So you don't think he loves you?

LEILIA. *(volcanic)* See? See why I can't stay here? Nobody says a thing until it's too late!

GOATMAN. *(unevenly)* Did I ever tell you about the first time I came South?

LEILIA. No, but I —

(*From his study, the* **DOCTOR** *now enters in incredulity at once again having had his quiet disturbed.*)

DOCTOR. Now I specifically remember asking for there to be no disturbances to my time this afternoon. What I would like to know is what all this shouting is supposed to be if not that.

GOATMAN. Forgive us, friend. We didn't mean to impose on you, but you know how it is to be young and unfamiliar to love.

(*The* **DOCTOR** *stares well-honed daggers at the* **GOATMAN**.)

LEILIA. Patrick was just mad that I decided not to go to the spring dance with him.

DOCTOR. I can't imagine.

LEILIA. I wouldn't expect you to.

GOATMAN. Perhaps I should go.

(*Stomping up the front porch stairs,* **GLORIANNE** *lets herself into the house. She in vain attempts to suppress her melodrama.*)

GLORIANNE. My stars! What is all this?

DOCTOR. Good afternoon, Glorianne.

GLORIANNE. Good afternoon, Doctor. Goatman. Leilia.

GOATMAN. Good day to ya.

LEILIA. How do you do, Mrs. Harris?

GLORIANNE. Oh, I'm just fine, fine, child. *(a beat)* Or I was until I passed by young Patrick in the yard. He was all kinds of miserable looking and wouldn't even tell me about what was the matter. I'm afraid you may have broken his heart.

LEILIA. *(genuinely saddened)* Oh, well. I guess I'll go and talk to him later.

GLORIANNE. Please don't get me wrong; I didn't come here to make you feel bad, even if you did break the boy's trust in all women. No, no. I just thought I might call on my good friend and his guest to set with me a spell this afternoon.

DOCTOR. Did you?

GOATMAN. That's mighty pleasant of you.

GLORIANNE. Well, I've tried to be a Christian influence on my friends and neighbors.

DOCTOR. So, Glori. How's the butcher business?

GLORIANNE. I'm not going to do this anymore! I hate him! I'm gonna kill him! I'll make it look like an accident! I could lock him in the freezer.

DOCTOR. Glori, please. Know your present company.

GLORIANNE. Oh, I don't care. I don't care. I just want to be rid of that man.

DOCTOR. Please! Take some calming breaths—in and out—and you'll feel better.

GLORIANNE. You know well as I do that don't do a damned thing! I'm tired of hearing your empty words. I don't even know why I came over. I should just be waiting at the shop until Harold comes in. I'm not fooling with you.

DOCTOR. *(cucumber)* Leilia, Ches, if you'd please excuse Mrs. Harris and me.

GLORIANNE. No, no. You may as well let them stay. *(beginning to circle her prey)* Doctor, you sit around in your safe house. You like everybody to know that you are separate, different from them. You just love being that big fish even if your little pond ain't fit to live in.

DOCTOR. I wish you wouldn't say hurtful things, Glori. I've only ever tried to be a help to my community. I only want to be of some good.

GLORIANNE. I'm sorry, but some things have to be said.

DOCTOR. I would like you to leave, Glorianne.

GLORIANNE. I'm really gonna kill Harold tonight.

DOCTOR. I don't care. Just go.

(She does so.)

GOATMAN. This is a mighty mess. Y'know once when I was a boy in Iowa—

DOCTOR. I would love to hear this story, Ches, but please save it for another more appropriate time.

GOATMAN. That I can do.

DOCTOR. I have much work to do and would prefer to be left alone.

*(**GOATMAN** and **LEILIA** exit wordlessly before the **DOCTOR** collapses onto the chair previously occupied by **LEILIA**. He sits for a moment as **PATRICK** approaches once again more the front porch. He makes to knock on the door, pauses, thinks violently for a few instants, and then retreats off from where he came. Lights fade.*

Scene 4

(As in previous interlogues, the half-light exposes the **DOCTOR** *rearranging furniture in his living room. He is thorough, dynamic in his actions. This takes time.)*

(From right **PATRICK** *re-enters unsurprisingly. He looks in the windows, then up to what can only be Miss* **LEILIA**'s *room. After gazing up to it for a few long seconds, he looks as though he will retreat yet again. The* **GOATMAN**, *however, appears before he can do such and, reaching to the ground, gathering up some pebbles.* **GOATMAN** *begins to pitch them at the boy then leaves just as abruptly as he came.* **PATRICK**, *having taken the hint, proceeds to toss them individually up to her window. This is done lightly, with care. It takes a few tries, but eventually he is answered.* **LEILIA**'s *voice is heard in response.)*

LEILIA. What are you doing throwing rocks at my house!?

PATRICK. I had to talk to you.

LEILIA. Well?

PATRICK. Well.

LEILIA. Well, what? You got me up in the middle of the night to talk to me. So what is it you have to say?

PATRICK. I'm not very good at this.

LEILIA. No one said you have to do a thing.

PATRICK. Can I just come in so we can talk?

LEILIA. We are talking.

PATRICK. This is important; I'm not just gonna stand in your yard shouting up at you. And don't play like you don't know what I'm talking about neither.

LEILIA. Fine.

(She goes down to lock the door, leaving **PATRICK** *to rehearse to himself what he will say to* **LEILA** *in a couple of moments. The* **DOCTOR** *notices her entering and crossing to unlock the door though* **LEILIA** *does not notice him. She lets* **PATRICK** *in. The room remains unlit.)*

LEILIA. So, let's talk.

PATRICK. Can't we at least turn the lights on?

LEILIA. I didn't want to wake the Doctor, but I don't guess he'll notice.

(She goes to the switch; **PATRICK** *goes to his spiel.)*

PATRICK. So as I expressed earlier this evening, Leilia, I think I am in love with you. No, I don't think it. I know it. Ever since we were—

*(***LEILIA*** *having found the light switch in the dark, the pair now realize they are not alone. The* **DOCTOR**, *however, is shown by the light to very clearly not be himself. He babbles and is uncertain in his movements.)*

DOCTOR. No, I'm sorry. I didn't mean to stare. I was under the impression that the hexagon was larger than that. I misjudged. My apologies...

LEILIA. *(worried)* He's sick.

PATRICK. What's wrong, Doctor?

LEILIA. *(more furrowed)* I've never seen him like this.

DOCTOR. They'll shine their lights brightly, briefly. They shine that quick light so that they can have the remembrance of the short flash for a very long time. A very long time...

LEILIA. *(trying to tend to him, to keep him from harming himself)* He needs help.

PATRICK. I still need to talk to you.

LEILIA. Patrick!

PATRICK. We can do that another time though.

(The **GOATMAN** *suddenly bursts in, obviously uninvited. He hardly peruses the scene for half a second before he takes action because he's like that.)*

GOATMAN. No, no. This all has to happen right now.

DOCTOR. *(taking notice of the* **GOATMAN***)* You! You! You did this! This is all your fault. You took her!

GOATMAN. We have to make things right.

(The **GOATMAN** *bodily lifts* **LEILIA** *and throws her across his shoulder. She is not happy with this.)*

LEILIA. PUT ME DOWN!!! Put me down! Let go of me!

GOATMAN. Shhh!!!

LEILIA. Put me down! I want down!

GOATMAN. What is it that you want?

(blank stares)

GOATMAN. Better question: Why?

LEILIA. Can you see he needs help?

GOATMAN. Who needs help?

LEILIA. My dad— *(She catches herself a bit late, then slowly continues.)* The Doctor is sick. He needs help. He needs me.

GOATMAN. *(snapping)* Doctors don't get sick! Doctors can heal people!

PATRICK. What are you doing? Put her down!

DOCTOR. No, no. The real doctors are too many hexagons away. Besides they have less spongy clients from whom to choose. I'm too well cast for them to pay any attention…

LEILIA. Fine then. Let's go. Take me wherever you were going to take me. I'll cut ties here and pretend I never saw that the Doctor is…. Let's go out on the road you love so much.

PATRICK. Leilia!

GOATMAN. You've done ready accepted this Doctor as your father. Now you can't leave him in such a state.

LEILIA. I can. I will. *(a beat, then to* **PATRICK***)* And Patrick, maybe one day…

GOATMAN. When I was young, I was closed off, too. Off in Iowa. Believe you me; there is lots of Iowa and not much to any of it. I couldn't stand it neither. I'd wake up early every morning before a soul else on our farm just to run out to the end of my daddy's farthest pasture. One morning I just kept on going. I didn't stop and I still haven't. But listen to me, girly, I tell you I ain't any happier for it. I could've been a simple farmer man. Isn't any of it good or bad; it's just different. I'd've put my kin through a good deal less worry if I'd stayed around, I know.

LEILIA. Then what are you trying to get me to do?

GOATMAN. See.

DOCTOR. Do you know what is out there? Past the mailbox? Past the next bend? Past the Wilcox Settlement at the end of town? There's not a city behind the next mountain ridge. No adventures, no adventurous people, not a hint of adventuring to be had past that doorstep any more than what's inside. What's out there is a bunch of green. Grass and jade and olive and moss and pine and spinach and willow. That's all you're going to find. Lots and lots of green. Green, green, green, and green again.

LEILIA. I don't know what to do for him. He's never been like this before. He needs help. Let me go so I can help him!

GOATMAN. I already did.

(*The* **GOATMAN** *sets* **LEILIA** *lightly down on the ground. She is unharmed. Unexplained as before, he takes his leave this time whistling a lilting tune as he goes.* **LEILIA** *dashes to the* **DOCTOR** *who has feebly collapsed onto the sofa.* **PATRICK** *remains a part of the woodwork; there is little to suggest that he will ever be anything more.*)

(*As the* **GOATMAN** *is making his final exit, he hangs a sign around his neck which reads clearly in bold lettering, "God Is Not Dead." The* **DOCTOR** *clutches desperately at* **LEILIA** *as he speaks again.*)

DOCTOR. I didn't want him to take you again. The other side of the hexagon is so far away. I didn't want him to take you there.

LEILIA. C'mon. Why don't you lie down now?

(*She helps him recline on the sofa.* **PATRICK** *fetches a throw pillow from the nearby chair as lights fade.*)

Epilogue

*(LEILIA and **PATRICK** are lounging easily on the front porch steps. Any discomfiture is so well ignored that it may as well not exist. They are silent for a brief eon.)*

PATRICK. Well…

LEILIA. That's a deep subject.

PATRICK. It's a deep object, too.

LEILIA. *(sighing)* So…I can't keep saying the same things over and over. Tell me a story.

PATRICK. Um…I don't have any stories.

LEILIA. Okay. A dream then.

PATRICK. You're always better at those.

LEILIA. I'm listening.

PATRICK. Okay…this is from a couple of nights ago. So there was this really average, middle-of-the-road, run-of-the-mill…ostrich.

LEILIA. An ostrich?

PATRICK. Yeah, an ostrich. Are you gonna let me tell it or not?

LEILIA. Go ahead.

PATRICK. So the ostrich comes to this stand of strawberries, and when he starts looking through them, he notices that one of them is extra shiny and just about perfect, that it was possibly the best strawberry that had ever strawberried. He noticed that the sun made it get little seeds all over. But as he looked at it, it sort of turned like it was fixing to get dark so he could only see its shadow. He even liked that a lot. They started to talking, and they talked on and on and didn't ever stop. And you could tell that the ostrich would always stay average for the strawberry and that the strawberry would always stay to strawberry for the ostrich.
And then I woke up.

(The two look directly out, wide-eyed. They remain so

for a time until the ice sheet is shattered by **LEILIA** *placing her hand on top of* **PATRICK***'s. He turns as red a strawberry as the lights dim to be as black as the under feathers of an ostrich.)*

End of Play.

EISEGESIS

Nick Mecikalski

EISEGESIS was presented in a staged reading as part of the Thespian Playworks program at the 2011 Thespian Festival on June 27th. Mark D. Kaufmann directed and Max Posner was dramaturg. The cast was as follows:

ARNOLD HALSWORTH. . . . . .Alexander Moll Johnson
MAN 1 . . . . .Jesse Beam
MAN 2. . . . . .John Templeton
DANIELLE RITTMAN . . . . Carli Rhoades

EISEGESIS was originally produced in The Blank Theatre's Young Playwrights Festival (Daniel Henning, Artistic Director; Noah Wyle, Artistic Producer) in Hollywood, California, on June 9, 2011. It was directed by Warren Davis. The cast was as follows:

ARNOLD HALSWORTH. . . . . Nathan Frizzell
MAN 1 . . . . .Gene Gabriel
MAN 2 . . . . Thea Gill
DANIELLE RITTMAN . . . . .Caitlin Eckstein
TIMOTHY . . . . Jesse Einstein

ABOUT THE PLAYWRIGHT

Nick Mecikalski was created nearly 14 billion years ago with the rest of the known universe as a gravitational singularity. After several thousand years, the energy that would one day be his consciousness cooled to a sufficient temperature for his atomic and subatomic particles to form, which then spent the vast majority of the next 13.7 billion years rearranging themselves into his conscious being. On November 28, 1993, this conscious being came into existence in Madison, Wisconsin. Since then, this complex arrangement of molecules has developed a strong affinity for acting, writing, and the unexplainable, and seeks to create answers to life's most unanswerable questions.

CHARACTERS

ARNOLD HALSWORTH – A twenty-something physicist and intellectual. Usually a normal, amiable college student, his given circumstances make him very defensive.

MAN 1 – One of Halsworth's mysterious interrogators; authoritative and intimidating but never violent. Measured and in control.

MAN 2 – Halsworth's other interrogator, of similar demeanor; may be a female role.

DANIELLE RITTMAN – Halsworth's wife, a smart woman with a dry and sarcastic sense of humor.

For those who truly put this play on its feet:

Mr. Dwayne Craft, Mrs. Mary Davis, Kaitlyn McClellan, Michael Herbek, Mallory Glover, Isaac Espy, Laura Hortter, Katy Sperry, and John Mecikalski

(Scene opens on a single bed—stark, blank, and white—set slightly stage left. The bed and about a three-foot radius around it are spotlighted by a lurid white light. The point at which the brightness of the bed area ends and the darkness of the rest of the stage begins is clear and defined, the darkness acting as a wall around the lighted area. At no point will **HALSWORTH** *"bump into" the darkness, though; it is nothingness—he will simply find it impossible to pass through.)*

(On the bed sleeps **ARNOLD HALSWORTH**, *dressed in slightly formal attire—khaki dress pants, button-down shirt, etc.—that is strangely in perfect condition.)*

*(***HALSWORTH** *stirs in his sleep a few times, murmuring unintelligible things. Suddenly a telephone rings, loud and urgent, startling* **HALSWORTH** *and making him sit bolt upright in bed and wake up with a jolt.)*

HALSWORTH. *(just coming out of a dream, yells ecstatically)* I'VE GOT IT!!

(His joy soon turns into confusion–he blinks several times, not yet completely out of his dreamlike state, not really registering his surroundings. Suddenly, as if remembering something important, he checks his pockets, which are empty—and, as indicated by his confused expression, shouldn't be.)

What? Where's my...? *(pauses; still not fully aware)*

(He blinks himself out of his groggy, dreamlike state, growing instantly confused. He looks around in bewilderment at this strange place, shadows of fear growing on his face.)

(almost whispered) What? Where...?

(Taking his time, he gets off the bed and moves around the cell, slowly and cautiously exploring and testing this bizarre new space, utterly confused. Once he reaches the edge of the lighted area, he reaches his hand slowly into the darkness, but is unable to move into the impossible nothingness. After examining the whole area, he realizes that there is no door.)

HALSWORTH. *(cont.)* *(under his breath; very much to himself)* Where's—where's the damn...door? *(called out to anybody)* Hello? Is...is anybody there? HELLO?! Anybody?! *(fear verging on anger)* HELLO?! Let me out, do you hear me? Let me OUT! I don't know what this is or what you're trying to pull here, but I know my rights! I know my rights, and I'll have a lawyer on you, whoever you are, and you'll stand NO CHANCE, do you hear me—?!

*(At this moment the telephone rings again, blaring and loud. It startles **HALSWORTH** into silence. On the second ring, **HALSWORTH** moves, searching quickly for the phone. Soon he traces it to his bed, where he pulls it out from underneath. It is an old, cracked rotary phone. He picks it up.)*

Hello?! Hello, whoever you are, help, please, I'm trapped in this cell— *(pauses, listening)* What? Who—who is this? What do you mean, "He's ready?" Is anyone there?! Listen to me, whoever you are! I don't care WHO you are, just TELL ME WHERE I AM!!

(He stands quickly, about to yell, but he stops himself, realizing as he stands that something is missing. He looks at the phone and with incredulity realizes there is no cord.)

(under his breath to himself; bewildered) What? Where's the...? How could I have...?

(Almost scared of the phone now, he drops it, shaking his head as if to clear his mind of this nonsense. He then begins to pace.)

HALSWORTH. *(cont.)* Okay, Arnie, nothing to worry about, it's just...just a dream, just a nightmare, these things always happen...I'm...I'm sure there's some...some Freudian explanation for this, of course, there always is...your subconscious can sure mess with you...I bet I'm...I'm trapped in my ego, that's probably it, and this is all just a release of my subconscious...*(beat)* Wait!

(He stops pacing.)

No, no, of course. Of course! It's a lucid dream. That's, that's perfect, I mean it fits perfectly, it's long, it's realistic, and above all I know it's a dream! Ha!

(Satisfied, he walks back to his bed and lies down.)

Now all I hafta do is wait it out, nothing wrong with that—

(As he is speaking, **MAN 1** *walks on from stage left carrying two chairs.* **MAN 2** *walks on next, carrying two clipboards, a strange, helmet-like contraption and a small handheld device resembling a calculator. Both* **MEN** *are wearing identical suits and ties, black and secretive. The sound of the chairs being put into place startles* **HALSWORTH** *from his bed, and he hops to his feet immediately.)*

HALSWORTH. *(startled; instinctually frightened)* Hey! How... how the...how'd you get in here?!

(His mind is suddenly buzzing at a million miles an hour— he searches wildly for where the **MEN** *could have entered from while at the same time watching them with a combination of slight fear, curiosity, and hope that they may be a way out and an answer to his situation.)*

*(**MAN 1** sits in the chair, while* **MAN 2** *stands to the side of him, slightly behind.* **MAN 1** *takes the clipboards, setting one on the empty chair. On the other he begins to jot things down.)*

MAN 1. *(without looking up)* Hello, Mr. Halsworth. Enjoying your stay?

HALSWORTH. *(not yet angry; still hopeful that they may have answers)* What? No! Now tell me how you got in here! Can—can you let me out?

MAN 1. *(to* **MAN 2***)* Put it on.

*(***MAN 2*** *starts toward* **HALSWORTH** *with the helmet-like contraption.* **HALSWORTH** *sees it and begins to back away, his hopefulness dissolving into fear.)*

HALSWORTH. Hey! Hey now! Don't you dare come near me with that thing, you hear me? I know my rights, you better believe it, and I'll have a lawsuit on you—!

(As **MAN 2** *comes nearer,* **HALSWORTH** *begins to push away.* **MAN 2** *doesn't fight him.)*

MAN 2. Don't struggle, Mr. Halsworth. It'll make this so much easier.

HALSWORTH. Don't struggle, what's—what's that supposed to mean, huh?! What—what the hell is that?!

MAN 1. Calm *down*, Mr. Halsworth. We wouldn't have taken the time and energy to place you in such a *fine* place of residence just to kill you, now would we?

(At this, the last of the hope that **HALSWORTH** *had evaporates.)*

Now, if you must know, it's a hyperelectroencephalograph—measures the event-related potential of a human with abnormally high gamma wave frequencies—that is, 125 to 140 Hertz—as well as protecting against catatonia, depersonalization, and other possible neurological complications. You might experience some discomfort.

HALSWORTH. *Discomfort?* Great, just great—listen, I...I'm not gonna play any of these science fiction games with you, okay? You're going to tell me where I am and what I'm doing here!

*(***MAN 1*** *starts up to go help* **MAN 2***.)*

HALSWORTH. *(cont.)* *(sees* **MAN 1** *coming)* No! No! I will NOT, I REFUSE! I want a lawyer! I want a—!

*(***MAN 1*** *grabs hold of* **HALSWORTH** *while* **MAN 2** *attempts to put the device on* **HALSWORTH***'s head.* **HALSWORTH** *struggles wildly, yelling the whole time about lawyers and rights, but* **MAN 1** *and* **MAN 2** *easily hold him still and place the device on his head.)*

MAN 1. Just be calm, Mr. Halsworth.

HALSWORTH. Stop it! Stop it, damn you!! I swear, I'll—

*(***HALSWORTH** *is cut off by a buzzing, electrical sound. His eyes are wide open as if he is being electrocuted, and his body is rigid with pain until he cannot stand.* **MAN 1** *and* **MAN 2** *sit him down on his cot.* **MAN 1** *walks calmly back to his desk and sits. The buzzing sound soon ends, leaving* **HALSWORTH** *a stupefied mess.)*

MAN 1. What's the reading?

MAN 2. *(looks at the handheld device)* One hundred thirty-five, sir.

MAN 1. Mm. On the higher end of the scale, there. How is he doing?

MAN 2. *(checks* **HALSWORTH***'s pulse)* Normal, sir. He'll be out of it in a few seconds.

MAN 1. Good, good.

*(***MAN 2** *removes the device from* **HALSWORTH***'s head, taking it with him.* **MAN 2** *moves upstage left, briefly placing it backstage and returning to his place next to* **MAN 1.***)*

HALSWORTH. *(gradually coming out of his stupor)* W-w-wha-wha-what...what was...was that?!

MAN 1. *(still jotting notes)* The hyperelectroencephalograph, Mr. Halsworth, I already told you. I warned you about the discomfort.

HALSWORTH. W-w-warned me?? Th-that was hardly a l-l-*little* d-discomfort! *(shakily tries to stand)*

MAN 1. *(without even seeing* **HALSWORTH**'*s attempt to stand)* I wouldn't try to stand, Mr. Halsworth.

*(*HALSWORTH *stands, then sways dizzily and sits heavily back down, massaging his temples.)*

Give it a few minutes, sir. It'll wear off, I promise. Now—

(He finishes writing, then gets up and walks toward **HALSWORTH**, *standing next to him.)*

I know what you're going to ask next, Mr. Halsworth. Where are you and why are you here. The first question is easy to answer, the second...well...*(beat)* Have you ever heard of the Pit of Tartaros, Mr. Halsworth?

HALSWORTH. The Pit of what?

MAN 1. The Pit of Tartaros. You see, Mr. Halsworth, the earliest Greek poets described the universe as a great sphere, divided in half by a flat Earth. Inside this Earth, at the very bottom of the soil, lay Hades, realm of the dead. But below that, in the bottommost pits of the sphere that was the cosmos, lay the Pit of Tartaros. This inescapable hellhole was so far into the abyss that Homer depicted it as being "as far beneath the house of Hades as from earth the sky lies." You, Mr. Halsworth, are in the Pit of Tartaros. Or, really, that's as close as I can get to it for you to understand. You're not anywhere that you've heard of before, Mr. Halsworth, and you're not getting out.

HALSWORTH. You've...you've really got a lot of nerve, you know that? Trapping me in this prison cell with no explanation for why, with no arrest, with no Miranda rights, and then telling me this long, fancy story about how I'm actually in Greek mythology—! *(stands in anger; steadies himself)* You tell that story to the judge, under oath, and I'm sure he'll be real interested in all that tartar pit crap!

MAN 1. I'm not sure you quite understand, Mr. Halsworth. You are not on Earth. You have no idea where you are. There are no judges, there are no courts, there are no lawyers, no *rights*.

HALSWORTH. Oh, you're so full of it—!

MAN 1. Then where are the doors, Mr. Halsworth, if we're so full of it? How'd we get in here?

*(***HALSWORTH*** *is quiet now; this has shut him up.* ***HALSWORTH*** *sits back on the bed.)*

HALSWORTH. *(not wanting to show his growing belief)* You're just messing with me....

MAN 1. Okay! Okay then, we're messing with you. So when my colleague and I leave in a few minutes, you just follow us out. I invite you. Just follow us out.

*(***HALSWORTH*** *groans, massaging his temples again.)*

HALSWORTH. *(muttered, to himself)* Jesus....This is insane....

MAN 1. Quite insane, yes.

HALSWORTH. But...this still explains nothing, you know. No matter *where* I am, whether I'm in some tar pit or whatever, there's absolutely *no* reason for me to be here, you understand?! I haven't done *anything!!* I—I haven't *killed* anyone, I haven't *stolen* anything, I haven't *cheated* anyone! For Chrissake, I don't even remember the last time I *jaywalked!* I'm just a graduate student, you know, I—I don't have anything against *anybody!* What in the world do you want *me* for?!

MAN 1. Good question, Mr. Halsworth. I knew you'd ask it. You must understand—this isn't a prison you're used to hearing about. You won't find a single murderer or rapist or thief within our walls. This place houses an entirely different type of criminal altogether, by far the most dangerous of all. This type of criminal would remain simply unnoticed back on Earth, ravaging his human companions without end—for he is not a murderer, rapist, or pilferer of the body, you under-stand. This type of criminal rages on an entirely different playing field—that is, the soul. This type of criminal is...*you*, Mr. Halsworth.

HALSWORTH. *(speechless, but then starts laughing to ward off fear)* You're—you're crazy, you know that? Like seriously crazy, off-your-rocker delusional, psychotic—or

maybe it's me! Ha! Ha-ha! Maybe *I'm* the one hallu-
cinating, wouldn't that be something? I mean, I was
actually starting to *believe* some of this crap, but then
you throw *this* at me? No way!

MAN 1. Don't worry, you're not expected to remember what
you did quite yet, Mr. Halsworth. In fact, that's our job
down here. To get you to remember. This place would
quite lose its purpose as a prison if you never knew
what you did, now wouldn't it? And, besides—guilt is
the best punishment, isn't it?

HALSWORTH. Yeah, yeah, that's just great. *(stands; tries to
usher them out)* Well, okay, you're done. You've told me
what I needed to know, thank you for your kindness,
next time you're in the neighborhood just drop by, I'll
bake up some cookies. But right now if you'll excuse
me I'm going to take a little nap—

MAN 1. You truly don't believe it, do you? You really don't
think you're here? You think you can just go to sleep
and wake up back home, don't you?

HALSWORTH. *(sits back on the bed, annoyed)* Okay fine, I
believe it. Will you leave now? I—I'm an awful person,
and I'm sorry for what I've done, and I'll try to change
my ways while I'm trapped in this tar pit for eternity.
Okay? *(turns away)*

*(**MAN 1** walks over to **HALSWORTH**, then pinches him
hard on the cheek.)*

HALSWORTH. Jesus! Ow! What the hell was that for?!

MAN 1. *(bends down to be on eye level with **HALSWORTH**)* If this
is a dream, Mr. Halsworth, then why haven't you awak-
ened?

*(Pause, as **HALSWORTH**'s sureness of himself falters in
his face.)*

Now—

*(**MAN 1** straightens and walks back over to his chair.)*

Do you know what year it is, Mr. Halsworth?

HALSWORTH. *(gives **MAN 1** a strange look)* It's 2019.

MAN 1. *(now sitting at his desk, taking notes)* Do you know who won the 2020 presidential election?

HALSWORTH. *(instantly, on instinct)* Cheryl Thomson. *(suddenly confused at himself)* No...no...I—I couldn't know that....

MAN 1. You're right, Mr. Halsworth.

HALSWORTH. ...No, no, I...I just got it confused....

MAN 1. But I'm telling you you're right. You couldn't have gotten it confused, because the 2016 election winner was...?

HALSWORTH. *(again, instinctually)* Arnold Sherrington.

(Not as confused this time; shocked as he visibly shows signs of believing.)

MAN 1. Exactly. It's actually the year 2021, Mr. Halsworth— that is, if anyone's keeping track anymore. You have some catching-up to do, I see. But that's not a problem—as I told you before, memory loss is a predictable side effect of the Pit, but your procedural memory has obviously not gone anywhere. Now—

*(rips off the piece of paper he was writing on and gives it to **MAN 2**)*

My colleague here is going to take over.

MAN 2. *(walks over to **HALSWORTH**)* Good day, Mr. Halsworth. I do believe we've met.

*(**MAN 2** extends his hand to **HALSWORTH**, who shakes it absentmindedly. **MAN 2** then bends down and takes **HALSWORTH**'s pulse. **HALSWORTH** is too deep in thought to notice.)*

MAN 2. *(to **MAN 1**)* Still normal, sir.

MAN 1. Good.

MAN 2. *(stands next to **HALSWORTH**)* Now tell me, Mr. Halsworth, what's the last thing you remember doing?

*(**HALSWORTH** blinks himself back into the moment. He is visibly tired from fighting them, but still reluctant to play their games.)*

HALSWORTH. The last thing I remember doing? Well, I—I guess that would be...well, I was going to bed...it had been a normal day as far as I can recall...just went to class, studied, a few meals in between, you know— normal stuff...geez, that feels like so long ago already....

MAN 2. And...this was all alone?

HALSWORTH. Alone? Well, of course, I mean I talked to a few friends throughout the day, but....

MAN 2. Hmm...because it seems that you've been married for the better part of a year, Mr. Halsworth.

HALSWORTH. Married? Me? No, not...not me.

MAN 2. Really? Then does the name 'Danielle Rittman' mean anything to you?

HALSWORTH. Danielle Rittman? No, I've never— *(Freezes mid-sentence. Abruptly stands after a moment in surprise. The hints of an impending grin grow onto his face.)* Wait! I...I do— She...she was a smart woman, wasn't she? And... and she had, uh, had glasses! Square, European ones, right? And she...she had the driest sense of humor.... And she couldn't sing worth a damn. *(gives a little laugh)* I always joked that, uh....I always joked that....I always.... *(blinks himself out of his memory, re-members who he's telling this to)* No. No, never mind, I'm—I'm just getting confused—

MAN 2. Just take it slowly, Mr. Halsworth, we're in no rush. Now, just start at the beginning. She was a... smart woman...?

HALSWORTH. I don't know...I'm probably thinking of someone else....

MAN 2. Just keep going, Mr. Halsworth. Where did you meet?

HALSWORTH. Where did we...? I—I dunno, I already told you I'm probably not even thinking of the right person! I don't even *know* this person, I'm *not* married to *anyone*, understand? You're messing with my head!

MAN 2. Mr. Halsworth, just start—

HALSWORTH. Bah! No! Stop that! Just—just stop saying my name, will you?! You're—you're messing with me, it's not 2021, you understand me? There has been no 2020 election, okay? Just stop!!

MAN 2. Mr. Halsworth, stop lying to yourself. You remember very well where you first met your wife—I see it in your eyes. Stalling this and refusing to believe it won't make it any easier on you; we have all the time in the world.

*(Pause as **HALSWORTH** shoots **MAN 2** a glare.)*

Sit down, sir.

*(**HALSWORTH** sits reluctantly.)*

Now, start from the beginning, Mr. Halsworth.

HALSWORTH. *(sourly)* Just...stop saying my name. Please.

MAN 2. Start from the beginning, Mr. Halsworth. Where did you first meet your wife?

HALSWORTH. *(Reluctantly; shoots **MAN 2** a glare. He then sighs, trying to remember.)* Well, I guess...it was...December, I think, and...she was...she was with a group of friends that I went to have a few drinks with one night....

*(Lights fade on stage left; lights up on stage rights, where **DANIELLE** sits alone at a table, nursing a drink. From stage left walks **HALSWORTH**, looking as drunken cheers ring from offstage. He gives **DANIELLE** an amused look as he sits down across from her.)*

HALSWORTH. Looks like we had the same idea.

DANIELLE. *(chuckles)* Yeah, and a good one, too. *(looks offstage)* Those guys...I love 'em, but...not when they're like this.

HALSWORTH. Yeah.... *(Embarrassed, as he realizes he never asked if he could sit.)* Oh! Uh, may I?

DANIELLE. Of course! I was wondering if anyone would join me.

HALSWORTH. Yeah, well, I've never been one for drinking...I guess I'm one of those lucky few who simply doesn't like the taste, you know? Wine, maybe. Not beer. Wine's too expensive to get drunk on, anyway. Well, *good* wine, at least.

DANIELLE. Or, maybe you're just responsible.

HALSWORTH. Ah, maybe. *(Grins.)*

DANIELLE. I don't believe we've formally met, have we? *(extends her hand)* I'm Danielle.

HALSWORTH. Nice to meet you Danielle, I'm Arnold. Arnold Halsworth. But don't call me by my last name, people tend to do that, and it just sounds so...so *pompous*.

DANIELLE. No, it doesn't! It sounds important. There's a difference. But I won't say it, pinkie promise. It is tempting, though. Sounds like a name of a...a CEO, or a banker, or a...a well-dressed business-man whose splendidly monotonous life fuels a growingly manic-depressive boredom until he leads a crazed rampage on his very own wife and kids.

HALSWORTH. Lemme guess, you're a writer.

DANIELLE. No, actually. I'm a storyteller. There's a difference.

HALSWORTH. There is, huh?

DANIELLE. Well of course there is! A storyteller *recounts* a writer's stories. Storytelling is just as important as the writing itself, you know. It's a symbiotic relationship—you can't have one without the other. What's a story without a storyteller? It's a bunch of words, that's what.

HALSWORTH. That's very true.

DANIELLE. You know Bob Dylan?

HALSWORTH. Bob Dylan? 'Course I do! "The Times They Are A-Changin'," "Blowin' in the Wind"....

DANIELLE. *(thoughtfully, with a far-away look)* Yeah. The best singer/songwriter of all time. Period. Well, he said once that "a poem is a naked person...some people say that I am a poet." I guess...I guess he saw it his duty to...to save the poem from nakedness, you know? And, well, I guess that's what I wanna do too. Clothe the naked words. *(chuckles)* Sounds funny.

HALSWORTH. No, it doesn't. Sounds poetic.

DANIELLE. *(snaps out of her far-away look)* And besides, I could never be a writer. Writing is such a *grueling* process. It's meticulous and aggravating and lonely....

HALSWORTH. Hey now, I like writing. It's...it's the most basic form of creation, isn't it? Creating your own, imaginary little universe. They say God was a writer before He made the Earth. Was a learning process.

DANIELLE. *(with mock seriousness)* Oh, I see. Was He a sculptor, too?

HALSWORTH. Sculptor, painter, sketch artist, basket weaver, everything. Apparently He was best at being a poet.

DANIELLE. A poet, oh really?

HALSWORTH. Of course! He perfected the art of having the most meaning while making the least sense, didn't He?

(They laugh.)

DANIELLE. Well, hey, I like that about God. He keeps us asking questions, by being so ambiguous. It's a smart move, too, because as I always thought, questions are the food for the soul, and without them, it would starve.

HALSWORTH. That's...that's very true. You're quite an insightful person, you know, Miss...?

DANIELLE. Rittman. Danielle Rittman. Not as important-sounding as 'Halsworth,' but I get by.

HALSWORTH. Hey now, Rittman sounds important! Better than poor Timothy over there— *(points to where he came from)* —Timothy *Schmidterton.* Sounds like the name of a Muppet. *(laughs)* Now, Ms. *Rittman,* being so insightful, what are you studying here?

DANIELLE. Mmm...I hoped you wouldn't ask that.

HALSWORTH. What, you still undecided? 'Cuz there's nothing wrong with that.

DANIELLE. No, worse. I'm...actually going for a *degree* in Storytelling.

HALSWORTH. *(shocked)* You mean you can actually get a degree in Storytelling? That's...that's awesome!

DANIELLE. In theory, yes, it is awesome. But it would also be awesome to, oh, you know, have some of the finer things in life, like a *job*, or *health insurance*, an *income*.... but either way, I try not to think about it. I'm happy blindly devouring the hard-earned money that my parents have saved up for the past eighteen years without worrying about the future. But enough about me— how about *you*, Mr. Arnold? What are *you* studying?

HALSWORTH. Me? Well, you'll laugh—

DANIELLE. I promise you, I'm in no position to laugh.

HALSWORTH. Okay, Physics. Well, *quantum* physics if you want to sound technical.

DANIELLE. Now why would I laugh at that? That's perfectly respectable! You could get a great job with an outstanding income, raise a few kids, become some famous brainiac like Stephen Hawking or John Nash—minus the paranoid schizophrenia, of course—publish a few books, you know, really be successful.

HALSWORTH. Yeah, well, I suppose. A lot of people, you know, don't look look on quantum physics very kindly, saying it eats up tax dollars and resources and all. But people fail to realize that quantum physics has done way more good for us than harm. I mean, who do they think rid us of our dependency on oil? The government? Ha! Of course not! But...but you know what really got me hooked in this field?

DANIELLE. What's that?

HALSWORTH. Well, it's this...this new theory that's being developed. It's the...the Theory of Unification, don't laugh. It's really hard to explain, but it gets its roots from the theory of informational reductionism, which is probably complete gibberish to you, I suppose. But really all it means is that the...the very roots of reality are information, not mass and energy. Quite a thought, you know? *(pauses, gathering thoughts)* But, basically, it...it ties everything together, this Unification Theory...I mean, *everything*, everything from here on Earth, to the farthest reaches of the universe, to what's happening now, to yesterday, to the beginning of the universe, to the *future*....

DANIELLE. *(after a pause, to take it all in)* Wow. Wow. That's... that's deep, my friend. And very impressive. I see you've thought quite a lot about it.

HALSWORTH. Well, yeah, I have, actually. It's really fascinating, it's...it's hard to take it all in, you know? And, yeah, it might just be science fiction. But there has to be *some* unreachable goal in your career, right? I don't tell many people that; most would get either bored or amused at it...which I guess is just as well, because if everybody found it as enthralling as I do, it wouldn't mean as much, if that makes any sense.

DANIELLE. Of course it makes sense! It's the same as with my storytelling crap...it wouldn't be near as special if it weren't for me being one of the only *five* people in the whole country getting a Storytelling degree at the moment.

HALSWORTH. Yes! Exactly! I—

(He is cut off by someone talking offstage who is only audible to the characters.)

What, Tim? *(listens, then rolls his eyes to **DANIELLE**)* Yeah, Tim, I got it. Designated drivers, pronto. We'll be right there. *(shakes his head in amusement)*

DANIELLE. *(also amused)* This must be the forty-billionth time I've watched them get thrown out of a bar! I can't believe any manager around here is crazy enough to still let them in.

HALSWORTH. Well I can't believe *you're* crazy enough to keep tagging along! *(They laugh.)* But...I'm glad you did.

*(They exchange a smile, then **HALSWORTH** extends his hand to **DANIELLE**, who shakes it.)*

It was nice meeting you, Danielle Rittman.

DANIELLE. Nice meeting you, Arnold Halsworth. *(realizes she said his last name)* Oh! Sorry about that, Arnold. Well, maybe we'll see each other around somewhere?

HALSWORTH. Yes, perhaps we will.

*(They smile. Lights down on stage right, **HALSWORTH** walks back stage left to the prison cell side of the stage. Lights up on stage left, where **HALSWORTH** sits on his bed, recounting the story. **MAN 2** has been taking notes this whole time.)*

HALSWORTH. *(actually smiling at the memory, his head is obviously caught in his past)* And...and then we shook hands and left, and... *(His reminiscent expression clouds over.)* ...and...and... *(He blinks himself out of his memories, the last signs of happiness melting off his face.)* ...damnit! I...I can't remember! *(His eyes still search futilely for the memory.)*

MAN 2. That's quite alright, Mr. Halsworth, you've done very well so far. We're not asking you to recall every second of the past two years, anyway...just certain parts. Now...do you remember anything at all about your relationship with Danielle after this point?

HALSWORTH. *(resignedly)* Look, I don't...I don't... *(beat, realizing)* Wait. Is she...is she *here?* Is Danielle *here?!* Did you drag *her* into this, too?!

MAN 2. I can assure you, Mr. Halsworth—

HALSWORTH. *(Standing now; faces **MAN 2** aggressively, ready to fight. At this, **MAN 1** rises, ready to quell a possible confrontation.)* Assure me of what, huh?! That she's *okay,* that she's only experiencing a *little discomfort,* huh?!! WHAT DID YOU DO TO HER??

MAN 1. *(Moves to **HALSWORTH**, pushes him back onto the bed easily. With forceful command in his voice:)* I can assure you, Mr. Halsworth, that we haven't laid a hand on Danielle. She didn't commit any crime, remember. We are an institution of justice, not senseless torture. *(moves back to his chair; sits, continuing to take notes)*

MAN 2. Now, back on topic—about your relationship with Danielle. Tell me what you remember, Mr. Halsworth.

HALSWORTH. I already told you! I don't remember anything, not a thing past that night!

MAN 2. *(doesn't believe him)* You sure?

HALSWORTH. Are you kidding? YES, I'm sure, it's my memory, isn't it? *(sighs, tired from fighting him)* Listen, you think you could just...you think I could just take a nap? Just five minutes? I mean, I'm here for eternity, right? Would a five-minute nap really put a dent in anything?

MAN 2. *(unchanging.)* I asked you a question. I expect you to answer it, Mr. Halsworth.

HALSWORTH. Stop it! Ahh, stop it!! *Stop* saying my name, will you?! Just, *stop!!*

MAN 2. If I stop saying your name, Mr. Halsworth, will you promise to remember?

HALSWORTH. *(shooting* **MAN 2** *a glare)* Fine. Fine, I remember. Me and Danielle...we—we saw each other a few times after that, you know, met up at restaurants, and she started doing these storytelling gigs at churches and schools...and...and, well, that's all I got.

MAN 2. You're lying, *Mr. Halsworth.* You remember quite a lot more, I can see it in your eyes.

HALSWORTH. *(groans)* Fine, you caught me, I remember some more. But you know you've got the wrong guy, right? I mean, does this sound like the life of a mass murderer to you?

MAN 2. We never said you were a mass murderer, Mr. Halsworth. Now, *continue.*

HALSWORTH. Okay, okay. Well...I mean, you know the story...we decided to start dating after a month or two, but to keep it secretive, like everyone does these days, 'cuz Dani didn't want the crap from her friends, blah, blah, blah, and things got more and more serious as the months went by, and, you know, we eventually chose to start living together, over at my place, but just temporary, you know, no hard feelings if it didn't work...and...uh...and...well, that *is* all I remember.

MAN 2. There we go. Now, do you happen to remember any details about living with Danielle?

HALSWORTH. Details? Well...no, I—I don't think I.... *(pauses, remembering)* Well...actually, I might remember *something....*

MAN 2. Something...?

HALSWORTH. Well, there was this one day, back in...back in...well, I just remember it was fall, I think...just a normal day, but....

(Lights down on stage left; **HALSWORTH** *moves to stage right in blackout. Lights up on stage right, where* **HALSWORTH** *sleeps disheveled on a bed, surrounded by textbooks and papers.* **DANIELLE** *walks on stage right, wearing formal clothing and carrying a large handbag. She sees* **HALSWORTH** *and smiles mischievously.)*

DANIELLE. *(bends down next to* **HALSWORTH**'*s ear)* Hey slacker, get up!!

HALSWORTH. *(startled awake, but still groggy and slightly mumbling)* Huh? Oh...Dani. *(jokingly)* You see, *this* is why I never wanted us to live together. I haven't woken up peacefully since you got here.

DANIELLE. It's what you get for being such a slacker. Sleeping on the job, tsktsk. *(eases onto the bed next to him; gives him a quick peck on the cheek)* Well, I am here and you are stuck with me. For ever and eternity. *(seductively)* Besides, you know what time of the day it is, don't you?

HALSWORTH. *(seductively)* Mm, I sure do....

*(***DANIELLE** *gets closer and closer to* **HALSWORTH** *until she reaches in her handbag and pulls out a cassette tape.)*

DANIELLE. Dylan time!

HALSWORTH. Right on the money.

(snatches the cassette from her, looking at it strangely)

What is this, a cassette tape? Aren't these like forty years old?

DANIELLE. Yeah, so? Still plays. Had it for the better part of twenty years. It's an artifact, too. Probably worth, you know, fifty, seventy cents.

HALSWORTH. Oh, yeah, a real keeper.... *(starts searching in his incredibly cluttered bed)* Well, the speakers are around here somewhere...How'd your gig go, by the way?

DANIELLE. Ah, successfully! They started out as just a bunch of bored Sunday School kids hearing the Noah story for the fortieth time, *(smiles)* but by the end they couldn't stop asking about all the animals. 'Was there an aquarium onboard for all the fishes?' *(laughs)* Precious. Now...you do know what this is, right?

HALSWORTH. What what is?

DANIELLE. This contraption we're sitting on. Most commonly referred to as a *bed*. That is, it's a device on which people usually lie horizontally to sleep. Not to be confused with a *desk* or a *bookshelf*, two very different household items, which store all your *crap*.

HALSWORTH. *(playfully)* Shut up. I was sleeping here just fine until one incredibly rude girlfriend of mine booted me out of my satisfying REM cycle.

DANIELLE. *(sarcastically)* Yeah, yeah, whatever, slacker. *(picks up a piece if paper from the bed, looks at it)* You and your Master's Degree. Where's that ever gonna getcha, huh?

HALSWORTH. Ah, probably nowhere, you're right. Maybe I'll just give it up now. *(picks up a speaker)* Found one!

DANIELLE. *(reading the piece of paper)* What is this, anyway?

HALSWORTH. That? Oh, that—that's nothing.

DANIELLE. Well, no, it's obviously *something*. This many Greek letters on the same sheet of paper mean it *must* be important.

HALSWORTH. Well, no, it's—it's not, really, it's just one of my little hobbies...kind of embarrassing, actually. You'd laugh.

DANIELLE. Geez, you say that about everything! What is it, mathematical porn?

HALSWORTH. No, it's—well, you know that thing I told you about, way back when? Like the first time we met?

DANIELLE. Uh...?

HALSWORTH. You know, the big quantum physics theory thing?

DANIELLE. Oh yeah! That!

HALSWORTH. Yeah, well...this is, you know, I've been...working on it a bit. But it's not a big deal or anything, just a hobby. *(pulls out the second speaker, trying to pull attention away from the paper)* Oh, here's the other!

DANIELLE. Now, why would that be embarrassing?

HALSWORTH. Well, 'cuz it's like every supernerd's dream to solve this thing. Most Ph.D's don't even recognize it as a credible theory, so right now it's the equivalent of a lonely teenager's quest to learn Kli-gon.

DANIELLE. Psh! This is *not* as pathetic as you're making it sound, Arnie. *(jokingly)* Besides, Klingon speakers are always the sexiest, I think. Why don't you explain some of this theory to me?

HALSWORTH. Oh, geez, Dani, because I can't even explain it to *myself!* Sometimes, it's weird, I'll get these bursts of inspiration, for just a few moments when it all makes sense, and I have just enough time to write it down before I lose it. And besides, you'd probably fall asleep. *(smiles)* You think we could just listen to Dylan?

DANIELLE. *(smiles back)* Fine. But when you solve this thing and become world-famous, you're explaining it to me, *capisce?*

HALSWORTH. Okay, agreed.

*(Lights down on stage right; **HALSWORTH** moves in blackout to stage left. Lights up on stage left. **HALSWORTH** is pacing, trying to remember. **MAN 2** still stands by his bed. **MAN 1** now stands behind **MAN 2**; the desk and chair are offstage.)*

HALSWORTH. Okay, okay, I get it. I get what you're doing.

MAN 2. And what's that?

HALSWORTH. This...this whole thing really has nothing to do with Danielle, does it? You're using your *powers of persuasion* to direct me to memories of this Unification Theory, aren't you?

MAN 2. We're not directing you to any specific memories. The specifics you remember on your own, Mr. Halsworth.

HALSWORTH. Gah! Ah! You're doing it again! That name thing! We had a deal, did we not?! I remembered! Now *you* stop saying my name!

MAN 2. You're not done remembering, Mr. Halsworth. Now, do you—

HALSWORTH. Listen, buddy *(or "lady" if* **MAN 2** *is played by a female)*, I don't think you quite understand what this theory is all about...it's not some recipe for a better *bomb* or horrible *pandemic*, you understand? It's...it's simply a theory that would essentially tie everything together...it's more for fun than anything else, okay? There wouldn't even be a practical application for this! How many times do I have to tell you, I've done *nothing* wrong, you've got the WRONG GUY!!

MAN 2. *(pause)* You and Danielle got married soon after this, isn't that correct?

HALSWORTH. *(plops back on the bed, resigned and drained of energy)* Yes, yes that's true.

MAN 2. And what about your studies? Your Master's degree?

HALSWORTH. Oh, the quantum physics thing? Oh, yeah, well you see, I got a little carried away one day and flew straight to the Large Hadron Collider over in Switzerland, bypassed security with a machine gun, and proceeded to collide the wrong particles and create a black hole three million times the size of Earth. Now, are you happy? Because beyond that, I don't see what kind of horrific crime I could possibly have committed in the past few months that would lock me in here!

MAN 2. Your studies, Mr. Halsworth.

HALSWORTH. *(sighs)* Fine. Fine. Well....I don't know, I remember little parts of classes here and there, and working on the Theory, I guess, but honestly...I don't know. I really don't. I'm sorry. *(pause; very sarcastic, his words resonate a rebellious lack of seriousness)* I mean, did I...did I solve the Theory? Is that why I'm here? Is it some crime to make progress, is that it? Huh? *(chuckles, amused at the idea)*

(MAN 2 closes his notepad, stands up, and walks back to where MAN 1's desk used to be. MAN 1 walks with him.)

MAN 2. *(to MAN 1.)* Well, our job is complete.

MAN 1. Certainly is.

HALSWORTH. What? Complete...? *(shocked, piecing it together in his mind)* That's...that's it, isn't it?! I solved that damn Theory, didn't I?! I—I can't *believe* it!! Jesus...! *(pauses, stands, realizing)* And...and *you* guys, you're just scared of a little progress, aren't you? *That's* what this is all about, isn't it?!

(MAN 2 walks off stage right.)

MAN 1. *(stands)* We're not going to answer that for you, Mr. Halsworth. We'll let someone else do the job.

HALSWORTH. Someone *else?* You mean there's *another* one of you in this godforsaken—?

(MAN 2 walks in, guiding DANIELLE. DANIELLE looks despondent and neglected: her hair is a mess, her clothes are dirty, she slouches when she walks, and she looks miserable. She is but a shell of who she once was. When HALSWORTH turns to see her, he is at a loss for words.)

Dani—? Dani? Danielle?

(runs to her, sweeps her up in a hug)

Jesus...Jesus Dani, you're here! *(His joy turns to grief.)* Oh, God, you're here... *(backs a step away, keeping his hands on her shoulders as he looks her up and down)* Christ, Dani, who did this to you, huh? Who...was it—was it them? *(pointing to MAN 1 and MAN 2)* Did you do this to her, huh?! Well, DID you?!

*(releases **DANIELLE**, storms up to **MAN 2** and tries to fight him, but **MAN 2** doesn't react)*

Don't you DARE touch her, you understand me?! I *knew* you guys were liars from the start!!

DANIELLE. Stop, please.

HALSWORTH. *(doesn't hear **DANIELLE** over his own yelling)* Do whatever you want with *me*, but if you lay one damn finger on *her*, I swear that will be the *end* of you!!

DANIELLE. Stop, please.

HALSWORTH. *(still doesn't hear her)* ANSWER ME, will you?! ANSWER ME!!

DANIELLE. Stop, please.

HALSWORTH. *(finally hears her; goes over to her)* What? Danielle, what—what is it?

DANIELLE. Nobody did this to me.

HALSWORTH. Wh—what do you mean?

DANIELLE. I mean no one did anything to me.

HALSWORTH. *(in a near whisper)* You did this to yourself?

DANIELLE. No, it's—it's what I *didn't* do to myself. I haven't *been* myself recently, no one has.

HALSWORTH. What? You haven't been yourself...then who *have* you been?

DANIELLE. *(sighs)* You were right. Very, very right. And smart, too. I always loved that about you, how smart you were. You were always so self-conscious, expecting me to call you a geek or nerd or something, but you know I never once called you that, never.

HALSWORTH. What? What are you trying to say, Danielle?

DANIELLE. The Theory. You were right. It did exactly what you said it would do. You said it would tie everything together. Everything from Earth, to the farthest reaches of the universe, to what's happening now, to yesterday, to the beginning of the universe, to the *future....*

HALSWORTH. *(stunned)* You mean...you mean I *solved* it?

DANIELLE. Of course you solved it. You're the smartest guy in the universe. *(beat)* But you see, I was right too, you know. I'm not near as smart as you, but a storyteller can be right, too. I said that questions are food for the soul, and without them, it would starve. Remember when I said that?

HALSWORTH. Yeah, yeah, of course! The first time we met!

DANIELLE. Yeah, well, your Theory...answered all our questions. We know the reasons now, we know all about God, we know what's at the other end of the universe, we know the fabric of love, and, most of all, we know the future. Our souls are starving.

HALSWORTH. What? What...that's just...just crazy.

DANIELLE. Sure it is. But crazy or not, we lost our reason to live, and, honestly, *you* took that reason from us: questions. More people commit suicide every day, you know, and honestly I don't blame them. Those of us still here, well, we've lost it, plain and simple.

HALSWORTH. What? No...no, you're lying to me, Dani, you're lying to me, that's not...not possible!

DANIELLE. Believe what you will.

*(**DANIELLE** starts back toward **MAN 1** and **MAN 2**.)*

HALSWORTH. *(holds her back)* No, Dani, don't go, please! I—I'm sorry for whatever I've done, I'll make it up to you! I'll give you a reason to live again! I—I love you!!

(leans in, tries to kiss her, but she pulls away)

DANIELLE. I have to go now.

HALSWORTH. *(on his knees, pulling her back)* No, Dani, NO, please, just please don't leave me here, not alone!! I—I'm SORRY, dreadfully SORRY!! Take me home, PLEASE!

*(**DANIELLE** walks to stand next to **MAN 1** and **MAN 2**; remembers something and turns around to face **HALSWORTH**.)*

DANIELLE. Oh.

(She digs something out of her pocket and hands it to **HALSWORTH***; it is the cassette tape from earlier.)*

Here. You might want this.

HALSWORTH. Your...your Dylan album? How could—how could you...?

DANIELLE. In the end, the poem will always be naked. It is beyond saving now, Mr. Dylan.

(starts walking off)

HALSWORTH. What? No, no, no, no!! Don't go!! Don't leave me here!! *(Holding out the cassette tape. Gets on his knees.)* Take it back! Take it back, I don't want it!! Please!

DANIELLE. Good-bye, Mr. Halsworth.

*(***DANIELLE***,* **MAN 1***, and* **MAN 2** *exit.* **HALSWORTH** *stares for a few seconds at the spot they just left, despair growing on his face. He silently looks down at the tape, then around at his empty cell, facing true loneliness. He slowly walks over to the bed, sitting down. Pulling the tape up to his mouth, he quietly begins to cry. Lights out.)*

PROPERTY LIST

A bed—stark, blank, and white
Two chairs
Rotary phone with cord
Two clipboards
Two pens
A futuristic, helmet-like contraption to serve as the "hyperelectroencephalograph"
A handheld device to accompany the "hyperelectroencephalograph"
Several sheets of paper
Two barstools
A small, round table
A glass or mug
A bed or couch to be cluttered with papers, books, pencils, etc.
A cassette tape
A cassette player
Two speakers
A purse

COSTUMES

HALSWORTH – Relatively nice clothing, a button-down shirt, khaki pants

MAN 1 – Professional suit and tie

MAN 2 – Professional suit and tie or corresponding female dress

DANIELLE – Relatively casual outfit for the bar scene; Sunday dress for the bedroom scene; tattered, disheveled clothing for the ending scene

SEE YOU SOON

Morgan Richardson

SEE YOU SOON was produced at a part of Thespian Playworks at the University of Nebraska, Lincoln on June 26, 2011. The play was written by Morgan Richardson of Enloe High School in Raleigh, North Carolina and was presented by the Education Theatre Association and *Dramatics Magazine*. It was directed by Carolyn Greer, with dramaturgy by Stephen Gregg. The cast was as follows:

GIRL. . . . . Rachel Shippee
BOY . . . . Adam Navas

ABOUT THE PLAYWRIGHT

Morgan Richardson, originally from North Carolina, is currently a play-writing student at Fordham University and a member of the Dramatist's Guild. *see you soon* is her first published work.

CHARACTERS

GIRL

BOY

They are both old enough to live alone

SETTING

Onstage, center, is a trampoline. To the left is a desk with a chair. To the right, a swing hangs from the ceiling. On the back wall is a blank white paper canvas that can be projected on. Scattered around the stage are pools of paint, all different colors, right in the path of the actors.

Scene 1

*(Lights up. **GIRL** enters. She is barefoot, wears a plain, light-colored dress, not white. Has a ribbon in her hair, as a headband or a hair tie. Black paint, or maybe an ink-stain, marks the inside of her left wrist. She's holding a few flat balloons on a string, the kind that once held helium but are dead now. They drag behind her as she goes and sits on the desk.)*

GIRL. I don't like water. I never did. It's too…unpredictable. I need to know what's coming. I need to know. No guessing games, no crypticism. And I guess that's why you scare me. I guess that's why when I'm with you I don't know. Know-it-all knows nothing, you know? I don't even know who I am anymore. I used to know. My favorite color used to be blue. My favorite day used to be Tuesday. Now it's like drowning, and up is down and down is up and I never learned to swim. Did you?

*(During this, **BOY** has entered. He's wearing sneakers; old, worn-out Converse. His shirt and jeans are also light-colored. He should give the feeling of clean. And normal. He watches **GIRL** tie the balloons to the chair, like a small child in a restaurant, and set about getting ready to brush her teeth at the desk, which serves as a bathroom sink.)*

BOY. Hey. Is this a bad time? I'm sorry, I just…I thought we might be soul mates. *(pause)* I can see by the way you're holding that tube of toothpaste that maybe you weren't thinking the same thing. At least, not right now. Look, I know I haven't known you for long. And I'll admit that sometimes I forget your name. Right now I'm thinking it starts with an S. But that doesn't matter. Well, I mean, it does. I'm sure it's a lovely name.

BOY. *(cont.)* But to me, it just.... I'm sorry to say it, or rather, I'm not, but I don't hear your name. Or maybe I do, but the tuba is too loud, and the trumpets, and the big drum. Like the Energizer bunny. And I hear that parade-cacophony of sound, and it's so loud and so alive that it beats right through the cement and into my shoes and my stomach and I shift and my heart doesn't beat by itself anymore.

*(***GIRL*** *studies* ***BOY****. She puts down the toothpaste and, taking out a pen and paper from the desk, writes "GIRL" in large block letters. She shows it to* ***BOY****. He smiles and takes the paper, putting it in his pocket.)*

BOY. So… Do you come here often?

GIRL. I live here.

BOY. Oh.

(beat)

GIRL. Do you come here often?

BOY. What a silly thing to ask.

(beat)

GIRL. Do you want to hear a story?

BOY. Is it a good story?

GIRL. No.

BOY. Are you alright?

GIRL. Why wouldn't I be?

BOY. I–

GIRL. Once upon a time there was a very frightened badger. The badger was afraid of the future. So she tried to think of how she could stop time. She figured that if she dug down far enough into the earth, she could escape time, because then nobody could tell her it was time to change. She dug and dug and dug until she reached an underground cave that time had left behind. She made herself a bed and a chair and a washing machine. And looked around and realized that she was all alone.

BOY. The end?

GIRL. No. The beginning.

BOY. That's a terrible beginning.

GIRL. Shh. It's not over yet. So the badger returned from the earth. And she stepped into the fresh air and was blind. *(pause)* The end.

BOY. I still don't like it.

GIRL. You don't have to like it.

BOY. Alright. I have to go.

GIRL. Already?

BOY. I'll see you.

*(**BOY** exits. **GIRL** looks around, bewildered. Throughout the following, she absentmindedly rubs the inkstain on her forearm.)*

GIRL. Once I tried to learn to tap dance. I figured it would be easy. I could feel the beat. I could learn moves. And I would be the best damn tap dancer you ever saw. I'd never fall out of step. And then I went to lessons and found out that tap dancing is just about the hardest thing I've ever encountered. It takes a ton of work. And a lot of falling. Falling and falling and falling. And then you think you have it, but you don't. You find your strengths and your weaknesses. It is so frustrating you just want to quit and never tap again. But if you work harder you get better. When you get it right it's the most rewarding thing in the world. And it clicks and you've learned the language and cracked the code and here you are. Here I am. I'm not the best tap dancer in the world. But that doesn't mean I'll never tap again.

*(**GIRL** goes back to the projection screen. She draws two people, like gingerbread people, almost touching hands.)*

*(**BOY** reenters. He has a few grocery bags and a cell phone in his mouth. He drops the bags and pockets the phone.)*

BOY. Do you want to have a picnic?

GIRL. It's nighttime.

BOY. Do you want to have a picnic?

GIRL. I'm allergic.

BOY. Do you want to have a picnic?

(beat)

GIRL. What are we having?

*(**BOY** smiles. He offers her his arm, and they move upstage and onto the trampoline, which should be raised above the stage. They sit, legs swinging over the edge. He hands her a small brown bag.)*

BOY. This one is yours.

*(**GIRL** opens the bag slowly. She pulls out a pair of chopsticks and a small box of Chinese takeout. **BOY** sets out his own box and chopsticks. **GIRL** examines her box.)*

GIRL. *(a little excited)* My favorite.

BOY. I know. I mean, I'm glad.

GIRL. How–

BOY. It's my favorite.

GIRL. And mine as well…

BOY. It's not so strange as it seems.

*(**BOY** hands **GIRL** a fortune cookie. She breaks it open and reads.)*

GIRL. "Sometimes, it's just easier to pretend you don't know what you're looking for, because then at least you know why you haven't found it yet."

*(**GIRL** looks at **BOY**.)*

I… I think you need to go. Really just go. Because I don't understand… well, you, or really anything anymore. I'm slipping. Slipping into ice water. Red alert. And my system doesn't know what to do with you, so before it becomes graft-versus-host… because I know the graft will win and take over and I don't think I can still be under all of that new. And maybe it would be fine and easy, but it might be awful and scary and lonely and I can't handle that. So before I get too attached to you…

(BOY silently takes GIRL's hand. For GIRL, it's like plunging a freezing hand into hot water. Slowly, she calms down and relaxes into his touch.)

BOY. You're beautiful.

GIRL. Me? Surely you're mistaken. Perhaps you are thinking about someone else…

BOY. You know I'm not.

*(The following overlaps on the bold words. **BOY** is earnestly trying to make his case, **GIRL** is desperately trying to stay safe. They are only half-listening to each other.)*

BOY. You wouldn't say that if you knew me. I want you to know me, and I want to know you.

I've got this… this feeling, and I don't know what it is, not yet anyway, but I know I wouldn't have it if it **wasn't for you**.

Don't you **see**? There isn't someone else.

Don't tell me to go. *(Pause. Smiles.)* **I'm already here.**

GIRL. You wouldn't say that if you knew me. I don't know that anyone really does, and that's why I'm still here. Incomplete. And I know that you think that we're of the same kind, the same puzzle, the same model. And I know that I could half convince myself that you were right if it **weren't for me**. I'm in the way and you won't budge me. I see your mind and you **see** mine, but I've got Technicolor lenses and you're crystalline clear. And unless you want to spin off into dizzy oblivion, you might as well just stop now. **Don't** make mistakes. *(pause)* **I'm already here.**

(GIRL tries to escape BOY. BOY won't let her go.)

BOY. Do you know what you are?

(**GIRL** *shakes her head, looking away.*)

BOY. You are the best kind of surprise.

(**GIRL** *looks at* **BOY** *and really sees him. Blackout.*)

Scene 2

(Lights up. The stage has been restored to its original format, with the addition of the people on the paper and the footprints on the floor. **GIRL** *enters. She has kind of a bemused smile on her face. She goes to the desk, pulls out a well-worn letter and a Chinese takeout menu. She rubs the menu on her face, inhaling. Her ribbon is gone.)*

*(***BOY*** *enters.* **GIRL** *does not notice. He sneaks up on her, puts his hands over her eyes. She feels his hands, and the ribbon wrapped around his wrist.)*

GIRL. It's you.

BOY. Who else? Hello.

GIRL. Hello.

BOY. Are you well?

GIRL. I'm excellent. I... I missed you. *(This surprises her.)*

BOY. Really? I missed you too.

GIRL. I don't think you understand. I miss you... more than every minute of every day. I see you everywhere. You're my everywhere. I see a toothbrush, and I think of you. I close my eyes and you're smiling. I count the breaths until you come back.

BOY. I'm here. I'm here now.

GIRL. Good.

BOY. I didn't...I mean...

GIRL. What?

BOY. Well, I don't know. I think I always figured...you're so independent.

GIRL. Or fake.

BOY. Never.

(beat)

GIRL. Pop quiz.

BOY. A quiz?

GIRL. Surprise.

BOY. But you know I hate –

GIRL. I don't. So tell me-

BOY. Anything.

GIRL. Favorite color?

BOY. White.

GIRL. White?

BOY. Your smile.

GIRL. Oh.

BOY. I'm sorry.

GIRL. I'm not.

> *(Another beat, a comfortable one.)*

GIRL. Push me.

> *(They move to the swing. **GIRL** sits expectantly. **BOY** pushes.)*

BOY. Would it be alright with you if I stayed?

GIRL. Stayed?

BOY. Stayed.

GIRL. Where?

BOY. Here. Around. With you.

GIRL. Yes.

BOY. Yes?

GIRL. Yes.

BOY. Ok. *(pause)* I have to go then.

GIRL. So soon?

BOY. Not far. Not far at all.

GIRL. Alright.

> *(At this point, starting somewhere in the above, they're touching foreheads as well as holding hands, with eyes closed. **GIRL** and **BOY** look at each other. Blackout.)*

Scene 3

(GIRL is lying on the trampoline with her head hanging off of the edge, toward the audience. She is reading upside down. BOY enters, a little perturbed and antsy. He goes straight for the desk, pulling an envelope out of his pocket. He begins writing a letter. GIRL looks up, and seeing BOY she moves into a more 'seductive' pose on the trampoline, still reading and trying to look natural. BOY is intent on his letter. GIRL waits for him to see her, then, finally:)

GIRL. You're back.

BOY. Hmm? Oh, yes.

GIRL. Where have you been?

BOY. Around.

GIRL. Alright.

(BOY is still focused on his letter. GIRL is becoming increasingly frustrated/curious. She stirs, shifts, readjusts. Her patience finally wears out. She approaches BOY.)

GIRL. What are you doing?

BOY. Nothing.

(He hastily covers his letters, guards them from GIRL's swipes.)

GIRL. Fine. I don't care, anyways.

BOY. It's nothing, really. Don't worry. *(He puts the letters in the desk. Pause.)* What are you reading?

GIRL. Shakespeare.

BOY. Really?

GIRL. *(still put out)* Yes. Don't sound so surprised.

BOY. I'm not, it's… which one?

GIRL. Richard III.

BOY. *(bursts out laughing)* You're kidding.

GIRL. I am not. *(BOY is still laughing.)* What?

BOY. Nothing, it's just… you would choose a history.

GIRL. You say that like it's a bad thing.

BOY. Just sort of a surprise, I guess.

GIRL. It's a great play.

BOY. I've never read it.

GIRL. Most people don't. It's supposed to be dry.

BOY. But it's your favorite.

GIRL. No, it's not. *(pause)* What were you writing before?

BOY. *(sighs)* It's just for work. Nothing major.

GIRL. *(lightening up)* Then why wouldn't you show me?

BOY. Because you're nosy.

GIRL. Excuse me? I am not nosy.

BOY. You are too. Don't even try to give me that.

GIRL. Don't be so ridiculous.

(BOY swipes GIRL's copy of Richard III and hits her lightly on the nose.)

BOY. Nosy.

(GIRL immediately goes after BOY and the book. A playful chase ensues, like a game of tag, all over the stage. It ends with BOY pinned on his back by GIRL, a la Lion King. A moment.)

GIRL. *(catching her breath)* You are a child. *(She snatches her book back.)*

BOY. So are you.

GIRL. Please.

(GIRL gets up. She goes to help BOY up, thinks better of it, and, trying to be dignified, walks over to the desk. She sits and begins to read again. BOY wraps his arms around her shoulders and reads with her. She's distracted, but in a nice way.)

BOY. *(after a moment)* Can I write you a song? Please? Something I can hear on the radio. Something you can dance to in the kitchen while you sauté onions. Something we can sway to at parties, or home alone. A song that would be a hit in a minute because everyone would know that it's true. I'd pick all the right words, and I promise I won't use your name. That can be a secret just for us. A melody soft and slow, forever. The kind you have to put on repeat, over and over. It would be a perfect song. Because I'd write it for you. What do you say?

(Without waiting for her answer, he pulls her out of the chair and begins to hum, to the tune of a popular love song. He draws her in and they dance as the music fades in under him. The lights fade to black and they sway. On the screen is projected a number of images indicating the passing of time; leaves falling, snow, rain, like it's footage from a camera taping out the window. A year passes. Blackout.)

Scene 4

*(Lights up. **GIRL** is asleep with her head on the desk, an envelope in her hand. **BOY** enters, sees **GIRL**. He has a flower in his hand. He walks over to her, lays the flower on the table in front of her, kisses her head, and leaves. When he is gone, **GIRL** wakes up. She is alarmed and confused. She looks around wildly, checks the letter, notices the flower. Gingerly, she picks it up.)*

GIRL. I was swimming. Nobody ever taught me to swim, but there I was, swimming. It must have been the ocean, because the floor was gone, and the water stung my eyes. I was trying to find… something. Something of mine. And I swam and I swam until I came into a cave. And it was dark and hollow and I couldn't find the way out but the only thing I wanted was… (looks at flower, then offstage, in the direction of BOY) and the mouth of the cave opened up and I swam out, and as I looked back over my shoulder I saw myself, smiling.

*(She begins to pull petals off of the flower, thinks better of it, and puts it in her hair. She reaches into a drawer and removes a stack of letters, read and read and re-read. They're **BOY**'s letters, the ones he's not showing her. She handles them gingerly, minding the paint. She tries to wipe a spot off of the one she's been sleeping on and return it to the pack when **BOY** enters. She replaces them hastily.)*

GIRL. Hey.

BOY. Hi.

*(**BOY** has another letter. He goes to the desk. **GIRL** goes to the swing, lazily swinging and eyeing **BOY**.)*

GIRL. Did you ever wonder…?

BOY. What?

GIRL. No, it's stupid. Forget it.

BOY. I won't.

GIRL. You won't?

BOY. *(playfully)* Forget it. I won't. It's going to consume my thoughts from here until Tuesday at least.

GIRL. Well then you obviously don't have much to think about.

BOY. Are you kidding me? That's an entire universe to think about.

GIRL. I guess you'll just have to Google it.

BOY. I'd rather hear it from you.

> (**BOY** *begins pushing* **GIRL** *on the swing. She's fine for a moment, and suddenly she's not. She jumps from the swing, landing funny on her ankle. She cries out,* **BOY** *runs to her, but she refuses help. She gets up and goes to the desk chair, shoving him off.)*

BOY. Are you alright?

GIRL. No.

BOY. Let me help you.

GIRL. NO.

BOY. Alright, alright. Are you-

GIRL. *(to self)* I dream too much.

BOY. I–

GIRL. Did you ever think about Pluto? Ever wonder how it feels to be Pluto? You're sitting there, a little cold, a little small, but secure. Maybe you're not really close to anything, but it's alright because you know that tomorrow you'll wake up and it's going to be the same old… until it's not. Suddenly they take away from you the one thing that makes you special, just like everyone else. And you're less. A grey area. And destiny is completely out of your control.

> (**BOY** *slowly approaches* **GIRL**, *like she's a spooked horse. She ignores him. She takes a piece of paper and a marker, almost writes, then realizes she doesn't know what to write. She tries furiously to remember.* **GIRL** *breaks down sobbing in the chair, sitting at the table.)*

GIRL. *(struggling)* I had something to tell you. I couldn't forget. I wrote it on a Post-it. I put it on my wall. Then in a book. Then in your book. You read it and smiled. But I forgot to add my name. And so I wrote you another Post-it. And I put it on my wall. Then in a book. Then in your book. And you read it and looked at me and smiled. And you put the Post-its on your wall. And I smiled. But the sticky was all gone and the one with my name wouldn't stay. So it fell. But you didn't see. And you taped up the first so it would never fall and promptly forgot my name.

BOY. Never.

GIRL. It doesn't matter.

BOY. It does. I know y–

GIRL. But I don't know you. I thought I did. *(Beat. With quiet intensity)* Are you going to tell me, or should I tell you?

BOY. What?

GIRL. I know you're leaving.

BOY. *(long pause)* How?

GIRL. I read them. I read them all.

BOY. You shouldn't have.

GIRL. So you wouldn't feel bad?

BOY. I was going to tell you.

GIRL. Were you going to write me a letter? "Sorry it slipped my mind, back in six months, keep dinner warm and cancel the paper."

BOY. *(quiet)* A year.

GIRL. A year?

BOY. I was going to tell you. I'm so sorry it had to be this way.

GIRL. Did you even try? Did you tell them you don't want to go?

BOY. It doesn't work like that. I have to.

GIRL. The hell you do! They don't need you, there's a million other people...I need you. I need you here.

BOY. I can't do anything about it. It happens. It's out of my hands.

GIRL. *(quiet)* Pluto.

BOY. I'll be back so quick, you won't even miss me. I don't have to go for another month. We can still–

GIRL. You don't have another month.

BOY. Yes I do.

GIRL. Not here.

BOY. I–

GIRL. Go. Now.

> *(**BOY** almost argues with her, but there is an undeniable finality. He goes to the desk and retrieves his letters. Without looking at him, she holds out her hand. He stares at it, hard. Finally he pulls her name out of his pocket and hands it back, folded very small. He hesitates, then touches her cheek. She flinches. He goes, looks back.)*

BOY. You're killing me. Slowly. So slowly. You say you don't know, but I know different. The writing on the wall is etched on my forehead for the whole world to see, but you're too busy staring at my shoes and my attitude and your fingernails to see it. To read what is only for you. People on the street pass me and hand me roses all for you, and you study my shoelaces and then there's nothing left of me and I walk away and you continue to look at the wrong sole.

> *(**BOY** exits. **GIRL**, who has been ignoring him, busies herself with trying to remove the inkstain from her forearm. It doesn't budge. She looks at the paper **BOY** has just given her and drops it in surprise.)*

GIRL. Who are you to be everything? Who are you to flip me sideways and toss me across the floor? *(pause)* Who am I to love you?

> *(Blackout. Projected is a photocopy of her name, except now underneath '+ BOY' has been added. Blackout.)*

Scene 5

*(Lights up. **GIRL** is cleaning up the mess, scrubbing fiercely. The inkstain on her forearm is much fainter. She fights with her hair, goes to tie it up but no longer has her ribbon.)*

GIRL. It's like being punched in the stomach, but instead of pain it's like your stomach just drops out, and you're all caved in and it doesn't change and then afterwards it's like you've failed to do something important. Like you forgot some vital appointment or something. Like a missed opportunity. That's what it's like when someone you love leaves. You see all these things around you, things you can't change, but somehow, some small part of you is blaming yourself for something small, something miniscule that you missed at some point in you life and you tell yourself that if you could have changed what you did, or if you worked harder at something you could change all of this but that's just your brain rationalizing, trying to make it seem like you have more control than you do and then it happens, and happens, and happens. Cyclical. Everything is a pattern, a cycle. Nothing is new. History repeats itself. We know the answers before we know we're looking for them, because we've already done this before. We follow the script, and play our parts, and when we're done, we're replaced.

(She finishes cleaning and surveys her work.)

*(**BOY** enters, very slowly. He is unchanged, maybe a little messier. He looks around, sees **GIRL**. He uneasily goes to sit on the swing.)*

*(She sees **BOY**, stops immediately. **BOY** jumps up.)*

BOY. I didn't mean to surprise you.

GIRL. Hi.

BOY. Hey.

GIRL. Do you need...?

BOY. I'm done.

GIRL. Done.

BOY. I… I had things to say…

GIRL. Here.

(**GIRL**, *still a little out of it, goes to the desk and grabs a pad of Post-its and a pen.* **BOY** *takes them, a small smile on his face. He writes.*)

BOY. I… am… back.

(*He tears off the top note and sticks it to the desk.*)

I… can't… stay… forever.

(*He tears off this note and sticks it next to the first.*)

Come… with… me?

(*This note goes next to the first two. He then draws a heart on the next note, and goes to put it down.* **GIRL**'s *hand stops him from sticking it to the table.*)

(**GIRL** *thinks. There is a long pause. Finally, she slowly moves her hand and takes the note. She puts it in her pocket. She never looks at* **BOY**.)

GIRL. Do you still have…?

(**BOY** *pulls an old, folded, worn note from his pocket, sticky all gone, with a heart.*)

BOY. It's not the one with your name. But it's still yours. Mine. Ours. (*pause*) You never answered my question.

(**GIRL** *glances quickly at the heart. She is very cautious.*)

GIRL. Could you just… hold my hand? Just for a second? Because I feel like I'm falling. Falling up. And there's no more earth under my feet anymore. I'm disconnected. I'm condensed. I'm so inside that if I ever come out again I'll surely explode into a million shards of paint. And I'll be everywhere and nowhere and I won't feel things anymore. I can't stop feeling. Don't let me stop feeling. Hold my hand. Tell me it's ok. I'm just out of reach of myself, a balloon bent on freedom. Jump for me?

(**BOY** *takes her hand, lightly. He guides her hand to his neck, and pulls at his shirt to show her a white mark, bright like the one on her face. Her hand rests on his heart.*)

BOY. I don't think you understand. I miss you more than every minute of every day. I see you everywhere. You're my everywhere. I see a toothbrush, and I think of you. I close my eyes and you're smiling.

GIRL. I count the breaths until you come back.

BOY. Because as long as I'm breathing there's still time to realize we fit.

(*blackout*)

CLIPPED

Sam Van Witter

CLIPPED was produced at a part of Thespian Playworks at the University of Nebraska, Lincoln on June 25, 2011. The play was written by Sam Van Wetter of Denver School of the Arts and was presented by the Education Theatre Association and *Dramatics Magazine*. It was directed by Michael Dahn, with dramaturgy by Judy GeBaur. The cast was as follows:

ELISE . . . . Kirsten Lynch-Walsh
PETEY . . . . Mark Devine

ABOUT THE PLAYWRIGHT

Sam Van Wetter is a high school senior at Denver School of the Arts where he majors in theatre. The writing and workshopping of *Clipped* has been a pleasure. He would like to thank his teachers, friends, and family as well as Dee Covington and the wonderful people at Curious Theatre Company for starting him on this journey.

CHARACTERS

ELISE is a woman in her thirties. She's prone to frumpishness and nostalgia.

PETEY is her parrot.

(The interior of an small apartment. Off right is the kitchen. Upstage is a well-stocked liquor cabinet. The perch upon which **PETEY** *sits is newly bought, as is the various bird accoutrement which sits, still in bags, by the front door stage left.* **ELISE** *circles her new parrot,* **PETEY**.*)*

ELISE. It does make sense. I mean, I've been on the look-out. Someone, a therapist, or someone, suggested this might, you know, happen. And I knew it. I saw you, you saw me. Made that instant, like instantaneous connection. Between you and me, between you and him. Or you and you, as the case may be, I suppose. It's a clever universe we live in, isn't it? It's so, so intricate, I guess. And rewarding. Or punishing, for you, I think. Not that being a parrot is terrible. It's just not a dog, or a dolphin. You know? Still a pretty little brain. Sorry, I'm sounding so, so rude. I've just prepared. Or thought about it, I don't know. I just, I want to establish that I want you to know that I don't expect you to feel guilty. Or too guilty. It's bad enough that you're back as a parrot, you don't need to feel like you need to do this whole retribution thing too. Is that okay?

PETEY. SQUAWWK. Quite.

ELISE. Hah! That's it. Exactly like him. It was that. That and the look you gave me. You winked at me, I think, and said "quite". Just like him. Or just like you. I don't know how to. Isn't that terrific.

PETEY. SQUAWWK!

ELISE. Goodness, sorry, I've been talking so much. Sorry, I uh. It's so hot. Can I get you anything? Water or…?

PETEY. Cracker!

ELISE. Isn't that right! You are so funny.

PETEY. CRACKER!

ELISE. Wait, seriously? I thought that was only in Disney and things, I've never really seen a parrot. Or had one, I guess. I was actually looking for a puppy or a kitten in the store, not a bird, I've been lonely and I was trying to. Uh.

PETEY. Petey want a cracker!

ELISE. Now, listen, I can't tell if you're making a joke. I've always had this borderline Aspergers thing, you know, Aspergers Syndrome, when you can't tell about other people and what they're thinking. I wasn't ever officially diagnosed but from a movie I watched I think. But I just am bad with sarcasm and I'd imagine parrot sarcasm is worse, right?

PETEY. Petey want a cracker!

ELISE. Good. You say it twice if it's a joke. That way we can differentiate, or whatever, right?

PETEY. PETEY WANT A CRACKER! CRACKER! CRACKKKER!

ELISE. Okay. Um, maybe, maybe you don't understand. I think you're being serious right now, though, so I'll. Uh, one sec.

(She exits.)

PETEY. Squaawk damn it.

ELISE. *(from offstage:)* I don't know what you like. Just regular crackers? I have rice cakes but I don't think. No. How about these, they're new, Nurticake? That sounds gross. But if you...

(She enters, offering him one. He refuses.)

No. Good.

(She exits again. Offstage:)

How about oreos? I don't think they're technically crackers, but. Oh!

(She returns.)

Stoned wheat thins? I always thought it was a weird name for crackers, this kid in my high school said you had to be stoned to think they were wheat. Or something. Munchies? Is that a thing?

PETEY. SQUAWWK!

ELISE. Oh, goodness. Sorry. You can tell I'm all flustered. Here. A thin stoner cracker for you.

(She feeds it to him.)

PETEY. Thank you! Thank you!

ELISE. Ooh! You are so welcome! Quite polite!

PETEY. Quite polite! Quite polite!

ELISE. Right. You are. That's what I just. Jesus, it's hot.

PETEY. Petey want a cracker!

ELISE. You keep throwing me off with that.

PETEY. Not joking! Toats serious!

ELISE. No, I know, or I think, but Petey? Really.

PETEY. Petey! Petey!

ELISE. It's so sad how much you've forgotten yourself.

PETEY. Petey! Petey!

ELISE. I would like to remind you. You are Glen.

PETEY. Petey! Petey!

ELISE. Glen. You are Glen. Please.

PETEY. Petey want a cracker!

ELISE. I'm sorry, I don't know who Petey is.

PETEY. Cracker! Cracker for Petey!

ELISE. No can do, Señor. If Glen wanted one, though…

PETEY. Petey!

ELISE. Glen!

PETEY. Petey!

ELISE. Glen!

PETEY. Petey Petey!

ELISE. Glen Glen Glen Glen Glen!!

(pause)

PETEY. Squawwk. Glen.

ELISE. Glen!

PETEY. Glen.

ELISE. This is wonderful. You're coming into your own. What do you want, Glen?

PETEY. Petey want a cracker!

ELISE. Ouch. Glen.

PETEY. Pleaaaase!

ELISE. Please what for who?

PETEY. Whom!

ELISE. You want a cracker or not?

PETEY. Yes! Yes! Petey want a cracker!

ELISE. Who does?

PETEY. Glen.

ELISE. Glen what?

PETEY. Glen wants a cracker!

ELISE. Glen will have a cracker.

(She gives him another. She studies him.)

ELISE. Do you feel any different?

PETEY. What kind of different?

ELISE. Like around me. Instead of the shop, or wherever.

PETEY. Why different? Why different?

ELISE. Well, because you're with me now. And we have this. You know.

PETEY. Don't know! Don't know!

ELISE. Glen, please. We've known each other a long time. And it's so perfect the way–

PETEY. Short time! Short time! Never seen you before!

ELISE. I mean, I guess for you, on this plane. Or this life, it's not.

PETEY. This life is the only life!

ELISE. Sure, that's what we all think during it. But for you, I guess. Your perspective. It's different.

PETEY. Oh no!

ELISE. What. Are you feeling memory? I've heard it can be painful and–

PETEY. Reincarnation is for crazies!

ELISE. Now, that's not fair seeing how you–

PETEY. I nothing! You everything!

ELISE. I realize it's difficult and scary to learn that you're a vessel for a soul but–

PETEY. Who do you think I am?

ELISE. What?

PETEY. Whose soul? Whose soul?!?

ELISE. Glen, it's clear that you're having a–

PETEY. WHOSE SOUL SQUAWWK!

(pause)

ELISE. You're my father.

PETEY. SQUAWWK DAMMIT SHOVEL IN THE ASS.

ELISE. Listen, Glen. I don't tolerate that kind of language. It's not fair, I know.

PETEY. Don't tell me about not fair crazy bitch!

ELISE. Excuse me, you–

PETEY. Get me a cracker, woman!

ELISE. No crackers for cursers!

PETEY. I'll get one myself! SQUAWKK!

*(With great gusto and enthusiasm, **PETEY** attempts to fly from his perch. His wings, however, are clipped and he falls feebly to the floor. There is an awkward moment.)*

PETEY. Damn wings.

ELISE. I can help you up–

(She moves toward him.)

PETEY. No! I can…

(He flops around on the floor and eventually lays quiet.)

(Long pause.)

Don't make me ask.

ELISE. Right. Sorry. It's that Aspergers thing…

(She re-perches him. Long pause.)

PETEY. So.

ELISE. I hate to say it, but you are sort of. Here.

PETEY. Helpless.

ELISE. And that's not a bad thing! It will be good in the end, Glen, Dad.

PETEY. Jesus.

ELISE. Don't.

PETEY. What do you expect me to do?

ELISE. I expect you to trust me.

PETEY. Trust you!? Trust you?!

ELISE. I realize that it's soon, but I know we–

PETEY. How can you know anything?

ELISE. I've got this feeling–

PETEY. Scientifically impossible! Impossible!

ELISE. Science is the easy way!

PETEY. Science is the right way!

ELISE. I know what I know! *(Pause. She collects herself.)* I'm sorry. I told myself I wouldn't get mad and that I would listen. I've done research; I know that it's hard, nearly impossible. It's nearly an impossibility for the reincarnate to be able to hop right into such a memory. Such memories. And I'm sorry.

PETEY. Squawk.

ELISE. I still am not ready to give up. I know that we have a deep and extensive relationship, we need to. We need to be open to it. Can you do that with me?

PETEY. Squawwk.

ELISE. I need an answer, Glen.

PETEY. Do I have a choice?

ELISE. That's not really fair.

PETEY. Do I?

ELISE. No. I guess. No.

PETEY. Cracker?

ELISE. Not now.

PETEY. Jesus.

ELISE. If we get through this. And you don't curse. Anymore.

PETEY. Squawwk damn it. Okay.

ELISE. Okay. I read somewhere or someone told me, or something, but recalling previous lives is much like amnesia. You might have the memories, somewhere, but they must be jogged. Reminded. In order to recall. So. Glen Allen.

PETEY. What?

ELISE. Does it, you know, ring any bells?

PETEY. Pffs. No! No!

ELISE. Okay. Okay. Allen Ladders. Your ladder manufacturing company. You were CEO.

PETEY. Nada! Nada!

ELISE. My mom, Jeanie. Jeanie Allen.

PETEY. Nope!

ELISE. Carly the goldfish. Gilly the gecko. Sasha, our dog.

PETEY. Nothin', muffin!

ELISE. Fine. That's okay. I've got more. It just so happens I've planned for this. I. One second. Don't go anywhere, please.

(*They both look awkwardly at his wings.*)

PETEY. I'll try.

(*She exits and quickly returns with a large file box. She sits with it on her lap and blows dust off the box. She removes the top and out spills piles of programs, diplomas, report cards, artwork, postcards, certificates: all varieties of paper paraphernalia.*)

ELISE. (*emotional*) Wow, Glen. Lots of. Lots of memories in here. Listen, this is. This is my prompter box. For you. I knew it would come in handy. It's my memories. My safekeeping. I've put everything worthwhile, worth saving. So I have it, so I can show you if you ever. You know. Re-emerged. Or whatever. It's. It's a lot, I guess. I don't know where to start. How about this. *(She pulls out a piece of yellow lined paper, crinkled with age.)* This is a poem I wrote for you. It was from middle school or junior high, I don't know if those are the same. But. Those were some rough times, I guess. Poetry, for me, was the best way to release. And express. Obviously, it's not the best, but. And I want you to stop me whenever you feel anything. Anything reminiscent. Or whatever. Just stop me. So. Here goes.

(She reads.)

Here I lay.

In the grass.

Which feels like water.

Or ice.

I am freezing.

If not to death,

To life.

To you.

To–

PETEY. STOP! STOP!

ELISE. What? Glen are you feeling / any–

PETEY. Stop. Wait.

(pause)

ELISE. Glen. Are you, are you remembering? *(pause)* Sure, yeah. Let it come. Don't rush it. Or. *(long pause)* Glen–

PETEY. SCREWDRIVER UP THE ASS!

ELISE. What?

PETEY. Shove it in her ARSEHOLE! ARSEHOLE! SQUAWWK!

ELISE. No, I don't need–

PETEY. SCREWDRIVER! SCREW DRIVE HER!

ELISE. Please, Glen, stop–

PETEY. You too! You too!

ELISE. What?

PETEY. Shut UP, woman!

ELISE. What do you mean?

PETEY. SQUAWWK DAMN IT.

ELISE. How do you feel?

PETEY. Like I'm gonna kill myself! Jesus!

ELISE. No, no. You shouldn't've. Don't interrupt unless you have something worthwhile. And I don't think that counts–

PETEY. My sanity? My sanity doesn't count?

ELISE. It's not gonna kill you to try!

PETEY. It sure will hurt!

ELISE. Jesus!

PETEY. No cursing!

ELISE. SHUT UP!

PETEY. Lady, you gotta–

ELISE. I don't gotta nothing! Stop! Squawking!

PETEY. A cracker sure would help.

ELISE. You are the biggest pain the my ass that I've–

PETEY. *(playing her weakness)* Don't talk to your father that way!

ELISE. What?

PETEY. Nothing! Go fuck yourself!

ELISE. Shut up!

PETEY. Make me, wench!

(She does so by feeding him a cracker. Forcefully.)

ELISE. My god. This is weird.

PETEY. Mmffmfss.

ELISE. Don't squawk with your mouth full.

(She gives him another cracker.)

It's just, even then, even in the heat of argument or, you know, you still sound just like him. It's exactly the way he would yell at my mom on the phone or. I don't know.

PETEY. Yelling?

ELISE. He, you would yell after you left.

PETEY. What what?

ELISE. Yeah, ran away. Moved to Argentina with some other woman.

PETEY. Ouch.

ELISE. Hah. I guess.

PETEY. Well. It's not me.

ELISE. I don't know.

PETEY. I do!

ELISE. Let me keep–

PETEY. No! No! No!

ELISE. Give it a chance. It's not that hard to sit and listen–

PETEY. I refuse! I refuse!

ELISE. Listen, if you don't I'll–

PETEY. SCREWDRIVER IN THE ASS! SQUAWK!

ELISE. No, you–

PETEY. I DON'T CARE! I DON'T CARE!

ELISE. You have to care! You're my!

PETEY. YOU'RE BATTY! YOU'RE BONKERS!

ELISE. No, no. You're being unreasonable.

PETEY. SHUT UP, WOMAN! YOU'RE CRAZY!

ELISE. *(shutting down)* Really?

PETEY. TOATS BANANAS! TOATS BANANAS!

ELISE. Oh.

PETEY. WHAT?

ELISE. Oh.

PETEY. That's all?

ELISE. I guess.

> *(Long pause. She stands and walks to the liquor cabinet, pours herself a drink. She then returns to her poem. Slowly, delicately, she begins to tear it.)*

PETEY. YES! Tear that shit!

(She continues to.)

ELISE. Maybe you'll never care.

PETEY. Rip it up! Rip it up!

(She holds the pile of shredded paper in her hand.)

ELISE. What a waste, right? It's not like I'd actually ever need this. Dead is dead.

(She then gently tosses it into the air. She watches it fall.)

PETEY. Trash it! Trash it!

ELISE. Beautiful.

(She takes another piece of paper and begins to carefully tear it.)

PETEY. Beautiful! Trash that shit! Trash that shit!

(She remains silent. She continues, methodically to tatter everything. She continues to drink.)

I don't care! I don't care...

*(Pause. Her despair and her alcohol inspire a kind of slow transformation in **PETEY**, a sort of awakening of **PETEY**'s consciousness.)*

I don't care.

*(Long pause. **PETEY** stands, unperched. He watches her tear her memories. He watches them fall.)*

DAD. Elise, hon.

ELISE. Yeah, try that. Hah.

DAD. Really, Elise. Hon.

ELISE. This was my first report card, Glen.

DAD. Elise.

ELISE. Straight A's. Lot of good that did.

DAD. Hey.

ELISE. Hey? Oh, hey, Glen. Didn't see you in my life.

DAD. Don't call me that.

ELISE. Right, I forgot. What is it, Petey? Petey want a cracker?

DAD. What?

ELISE. What does Daddy want? A cracker? A daughter? Hah.

DAD. Stop it.

ELISE. Really, Glen. Unbelievable.

DAD. Call me Dad.

ELISE. Unbelievable.

DAD. Really.

ELISE. Oh, and this is my Diversity Awareness Certificate. You were always good with diversity, weren't you, Glen? Love those South Americans.

DAD. Please, Elise.

ELISE. Right, because "Dad" is less harsh, I'd be–

DAD. I'm not asking you to be nice to me.

ELISE. Good. Not happening.

DAD. Just, please. Acknowledge me. As a. I don't know. A person.

ELISE. You, my idiot reincarnated bird.

DAD. Elise. Look at me.

ELISE. And here we have a picture I drew of you and me. Not too bad, considering it was drawn from my imagination.

DAD. Ellie. Give me that.

ELISE. Don't. Call me that.

DAD. Please, I'd like to see–

ELISE. See how fucked up I am? How lonely, how. Really, what were you thinking, coming here.

DAD. I don't know, hon. Amends.

ELISE. Right. I'd like to see you make anything right.

DAD. Consider this a first.

ELISE. Consider this a failure.

DAD. Consider it a test.

ELISE. Unbelievable.

DAD. Ellie. Look at me.

(She does so for the first time since his transfiguration. It's a shock; his parrot self is abandoned completely. He smiles sadly.

Hey.

ELISE. *(shocked at the leaps her mind has taken)* Oh my god. Oh, hi. I mean. Um. Sorry. I just expected, I don't know. More drills in the ass or something.

DAD. What?

ELISE. Uh, never mind. I, uh. Never mind.

DAD. What are you working on?

ELISE. This picture.

DAD. That's me?

ELISE. Yeah.

DAD. I'm really tall.

ELISE. And you don't have fingers. Sorry I–

DAD. You were young. Yeah.

ELISE. Yeah.

(pause)

DAD. How's your mother?

ELISE. She's okay.

DAD. Is she around or…?

(He gestures vaguely offstage.)

ELISE. She's in a home now, actually.

DAD. Sick of the apartment then?

ELISE. Like an assisted living home.

DAD. Oh. Oh, I'm so sorry. Do you need–

ELISE. Insurance is paying for it.

DAD. Right. *(pause)* What happened?

ELISE. She tried to kill herself. Twice.

DAD. I'm so sorry, that sounds–

ELISE. It is. Was. It's okay.

DAD. So. What are you doing?

ELISE. I was ripping this stuff up.

DAD. Oh. I mean, no. Like in your life. Are you working? Or…

ELISE. Oh. Uh, some, well, some freelance editing. And things. I'm trying to open up my own business, though.

DAD. What sort?

ELISE. *(scrambling, inspired by her recent purchases)* I, uh, I'm thinking birds. Bird breeding and boarding, that sort of thing.

DAD. Neat.

ELISE. Yeah, it's okay. It's interesting.

DAD. I don't know if you knew, but I had some birds in Buenos Aires.

ELISE. Oh.

DAD. My girls liked them.

ELISE. I'm sure.

(Long pause. Awkward.)

DAD. Listen, hon, I want to…

ELISE. It's okay.

DAD. I know it was awhile ago, but I want you–

ELISE. Really, Glen, you don't–

DAD. Will you stop that?

ELISE. What?

DAD. I want to be your father, Elise. Ellie.

ELISE. I know, Glen, Dad, but now, you can't–

DAD. I know. But I want to try. I want to. I don't know. To pay retribution and atone. I want to be here when you need me, whenever you need me.

ELISE. And now is a good time to start?

DAD. It's not optimal, I know, but it's better than, well–

ELISE. I get it.

DAD. You do?

ELISE. Yeah.

DAD. Do you… do you want me to?

ELISE. I don't know.

DAD. Okay.

(pause)

ELISE. Do you want something to drink?

DAD. Yeah.

(She goes to the liquor cabinet, tops her own glass off then pours him some as well.)

(pause)

ELISE. What were they like?

DAD. What?

ELISE. Your… you know. Your other family.

DAD. Don't put it like that.

ELISE. I know, I just. I just realized I don't even know their names, much less / how they–

DAD. They were kind. They were different. You know that your mother and I have known each other since we were 16? 16. That's so young, so…

ELISE. I can't imagine it.

DAD. I know. And she, Letta, I mean, was so–

ELISE. Letta?

DAD. Yeah. My second– my other.

ELISE. Letta.

DAD. What?

ELISE. I just pictured her differently.

DAD. I mean, you don't really know her or–

ELISE. I know, sorry. I just pictured an Alejandra or a Guadalupe. It's nothing–

DAD. She's Russian, actually.

ELISE. Oh.

DAD. Her husband was the Argentinean.

ELISE. So you both were–

DAD. Yeah. It was sorta, well–

ELISE. Equal. Equal hurt.

DAD. I don't know.

(pause)

ELISE. You had daughters?

DAD. Yes. Two. Beautiful, beautiful girls.

ELISE. Oh. *(pause)* Did it seem like a good idea?

DAD. What?

ELISE. I mean, to you. At the time.

DAD. I, uh, I don't know. I guess so, yeah. It always does, at the time.

ELISE. Does it– does it still?

DAD. I don't know. Yes in so many ways. No in many more.

ELISE. Really?

DAD. But, Ellie, hon. I'm ready to put that, you know, behind us. I'm ready to move on. I want to be here with you, for you. I want to finally get to know you. To make amends.

ELISE. You already said that.

DAD. I know, but I really mean what. What I mean is–

ELISE. I don't know, Dad.

DAD. What.

ELISE. I mean, at this point. It– It's so weird.

DAD. What, hon?

ELISE. I've pictured this forever. I've thought it over, I've prepared for this moment, I mean, you saw my box of memories! And now, now you're here, you're, you're. I don't know. It doesn't seem like. I don't know.

DAD. No, no. What do you want? I can do what you need, I can. I just want to.

ELISE. What do I want? I want the freedom you had. I want the ability to up and walk away from all this... this shit. I want to meet a Russian man and take him from his beautiful wife and have babies with him! I want to be young, to let my belly expand into shining little boys and girls. I want those years back, those years when you left me with my devastated mother and the occasional alimony check. But I don't want to be you. No. I want anything but you, your traits. I want to unsee all those similarities between us, the love for a good scotch, the aversion to commitment. I want to be alone, elsewhere, with all this behind me. I want to go to sleep at night, even just one night, and feel satisfied with myself. I want purpose, I want love. I want to say this. I want closure. But I don't want you.

DAD. Ellie, hon. I can help, I can–

ELISE. *(It's the first time in her life she's had permission to say no to him.)* You can't, Dad. It's not you. It's not your fault. It's me. It sounds so. But I just realized, everything I've known, nearly everything, has been without you. You've been dead to me, biologically, figuratively, for so long. A lifetime. I've struggled so much to learn to survive, to exist, I can't have to relearn. And you can't reteach.

DAD. I can still help, though, right? I can do more than ever before. Can't I…

ELISE. I just think that you– it's not now that we need each other. Thank you, I guess, for helping me to know what I've known all along, but it's not enough. It's not worth it.

DAD. It's. That's okay. It makes sense, it's okay. It just seemed that, you know, whenever would be good for me would be good for you.

ELISE. You've always thought that.

DAD. I know. I'm sorry, I'm so.

ELISE. It's okay, Dad.

(Pause. Long pause.)

DAD. Ellie, hon.

ELISE. Dad.

DAD. Will you dance with me?

ELISE. I don't know.

DAD. Please. It's the least you can do. Please.

ELISE. Okay. Kay.

*(They dance, slowly, sadly. She stretches to kiss him on the cheek. Her temporary dream ends and he disappears. She kisses air. She doesn't mind. She continues to waltz as **PETEY** returns to his perch. Her eyes are shut.)*

PETEY. *(awakening her from her reverie)* Pretty lady! Pretty lady!

ELISE. Dad. Thank you for…

PETEY. Hello hello! Hello hello!

ELISE. Absolutely, I understand. I think I'll be… I think I'm able to…

PETEY. SQUAWWK! Loco lady! Loco lady! Phoning home!!

ELISE. Petey! One second. I'm saying good-bye…

PETEY. And I'm saying that I'm hungry! And you're crazy! You're crazy!

ELISE. I think I'm able to. To forgive. Not forgive you. Forgive the idea of you.

PETEY. Petey wants a cracker! Cracker!

ELISE. A moment, Petey…

PETEY. An institution, nutso!

ELISE. Glen, Dad, listen…

PETEY. Listenin', loony pie!

ELISE. No, I was talking to my Dad, Petey…

PETEY. Petey or Glen! Make up your marbles!

ELISE. You. Petey. A moment…

PETEY. SSQUUAWK!

(*Slowly,* ELISE *opens her eyes. She sees* PETEY.)

ELISE. Let's see about that cracker, hmm? A moment, Dad–

(*She turns to where she stopped dancing. She sees no one. She smiles.*)

A… a moment.

(*She waltzes with a cracker to* PETEY. *She feeds it to him. She opens the front door and moves him next to it. She waltzes offstage.*)

(*Curtain.*)

OTHER TITLES AVAILABLE FROM SAMUEL FRENCH

THESPIAN PLAYWORKS 2010

Various Authors

Short Plays / Various Casting

A princess. A professor. A teen-aged mother. A fugitive on the run from all forms of social media.

From the nationally recognized Educational Theatre Association's Thespian Playworks competition come four short scripts with unforgettable heroes – all created by high school-aged playwrights! Included in this volume are:

A Backwards Fairytale by Allie Lehnhoff
In Facebook Wii Trust by Lien Le
The Porcelain Vase by Christopher Poore
Splinters by Meg Bradley

These winning plays were selected from a wide pool of national applicants, and represent some of the most exciting new work by young playwrights across the country.

OTHER TITLES AVAILABLE FROM SAMUEL FRENCH

KEN LUDWIG'S MIDSUMMER/JERSEY

Ken Ludwig

Comedy, Adaptation / 5m, 10f-22f

Ken Ludwig's Midsummer/Jersey is the hilarious high-octane re-telling of Shakespeare's *Midsummer Night's Dream* set on the boardwalk of a seaside town in modern-day New Jersey. The story is set into motion by the impending marriage of the Governor of New Jersey, the love affairs of four beach-bound high school crushes, a lively crew of fairies and the staff of the local beauty salon (run by Patti Quince and Stylist Nikki Bottom). The night takes a magical, mayhem-filled turn when Oberon–angered by his wife who refuses to buy him a muscle car for his birthday–and the impish Puck arrive on the scene armed with a powerful love-potion-filled flower and a desire for mischief making. With several weddings and the acting careers of six beauticians hanging in the balance, the lovers take to the boardwalk, backed by pop music and an iPhone-obsessed wood sprite. Written for high schools and colleges, *Midsummer/Jersey* received its world premiere in November 2011 at James Robinson High School in Fairfax, VA where it played to sold-out houses.

"A seamless blend of MTV reality show Jersey Shore and Shakespeare's *A Midsummer Night's Dream*... with fresh, poetic dialogue, frequent recitations of authentic quotes, and countless pop culture references." *– Fairfax Connection*

"Appealing to the cultural tastes and theatrical ambitions of the [next] generation" *– The Washington Post*

"A sensational jest of pop culture and examines the test of true love... An explosive combination of brassy personalities and bold hilarity" *– Fairfax Station Patch*

OTHER TITLES AVAILABLE FROM SAMUEL FRENCH

ELEPHANT'S GRAVEYARD

George Brant

Drama / 10m, 3f, flexible casting (Roles may be played by any race or gender except when specified.)

Winner of the 2008 Keene Prize for Literature
Winner of the 2008 David Mark Cohen National Playwriting Award

Elephant's Graveyard is the true tale of the tragic collision of a struggling circus and a tiny town in Tennessee, which resulted in the only known lynching of an elephant. Set in September of 1916, the play combines historical fact and legend, exploring the deep-seated American craving for spectacle, violence and revenge.

"The script—based on a true story about a traveling circus that, in 1916, stumbled into gory disaster in a muddy Tennessee town—is, like the best art, microscopically specific with echoes that radiate outward across time. It conjures a world with its own atmosphere and terrible internal logic. It's mesmerizing... symphonic in its emotional variations on a tragic theme. *Elephant's Graveyard* buzzes with truth about the consequences of misunderstanding, the invisible but enormous gap between artists and their audiences, and the infernal beauty of vaudeville."
– *The Stranger, Seattle*

"A theatrical masterpiece."
– *Columbia City Paper*

"The most striking production in the (NSDF) festival."
– *Times of London*

"Deeply moving…has the audience in stitches at the open and tears at the close."
– *TheSunCoast.com*

OTHER TITLES AVAILABLE FROM SAMUEL FRENCH

MIRROR MIRROR

Sarah Treem

Dramatic Comedy / 5m, 5f

"Roy, is this a dream?

A dream, a story, high school, insanity. It's hard to tell sometimes, isn't it?"

A high school Homecoming dance in the south. In the bathroom Gretchen Black, the most popular girl in school, lights a cigarette and asks the mirror on the wall who's the fairest of them all. The mirror shows her a horrible witch instead of her own reflection. Gretchen puts the cigarette out in her armpit and the witch disappears. Moments later a mysterious new girl named Rose White arrives at Homecoming. She has no hips or chest to speak of, but her skin shines white as snow and her lips are as red as the rose. She's after Gretchen's boyfriend, Badger Biers. In this dark comedy, based on Snow White, ten teenagers love, lose, betray and revenge each other over one autumnal weekend in a kingdom far, far away. It is a precarious landscape where magic lurks behind make-up, mirrors and memories.